THE DEEPEST BLUE

ROADMAP TO YOUR HEART, BOOK #3

CHRISTINA LEE

For A.

1

DEAN

I lugged my bike through the door and propped it against the wall. Sliding my messenger bag over my sore shoulder, I sank down on the couch, attempting to take a load off.

Spring semester had finally kicked my ass. I was working tons of hours at one of the labs in the biology department in addition to coping with my regular coursework for my master's program. But I only needed one more intensive summer class to graduate early.

I rummaged around in my bag for my laptop, but when I found it I didn't bother to turn it on. I was too beat to work on any more homework tonight.

A couple minutes later, my roommate, Cassie, hustled through the door. She was juggling an armload of textbooks and I sprang up to help.

"He keep you after class again?" I smirked as I placed her books on the table that we used as much for storage as for eating. Though lately, between both our schedules, there wasn't even enough time for us to share a meal.

"Nope." She strode to the refrigerator to retrieve a cold drink. "I asked if he needed help."

Cassie was a professor's assistant and refused to admit her crush on the handsome and neurotic Dr. Rebol. She'd graduate early as well, but not until winter break.

I braced my hands on her shoulders to give her a quick massage. She rolled her neck as my fingers worked her tense muscles. "The kind of help that involves you being down on your knees?"

She laughed, elbowing me lightly in the ribs. "That's your fantasy, not mine."

"Probably right." I sighed and settled back on the couch.

Maybe I needed to get laid. It'd been a few weeks. But I didn't have the energy to change out of my khakis and button-down to head to the club tonight.

"Let's open a bottle of white." Cassie set her water container on the table and headed to her room to change.

This had become our routine on the nights we were both home. Otherwise, we'd end up on opposite ends of our two-bed and two-bath apartment. We'd been living in this refurbished building in Cameron Village for more than a year, while we finished up at NC State. She wanted to teach business to under-grads and I was eager to be more than a research assistant.

On some base level, I also hoped to earn my father's approval. Maybe then he'd actually give a damn. He would've preferred for me to follow in his footsteps. I could've had a marketing job waiting for me upon graduation. Though he never admitted it openly, he questioned whether I could make it in a field that relied heavily on grants and donations, all in the name of science and improving the earth.

"That's better." Cassie had thrown on her favorite pastel pajamas with bold red hearts, the only time she showcased her love of bright and puffy designs. Having grown up with three brothers on a game preserve in Florida, she was definitely a tough cookie, but I liked when her softer side showed.

I handed her a glass of Chardonnay and we got comfortable

on the cushions. We'd become good friends these past few months, having met last year through a roommate posting board in student services. Both transplants from our hometowns, our families were conservative in different ways.

Her brothers were hunky country types who rode around on ATVs—I'd seen photos and some of the images still got my pulse pumping. My family was just plain stuffy in comparison with their dinner parties and charity events. Except for my half-brother, Felix, who I connected with when I'd gotten my undergraduate degree.

We shared the same mother but that was about all we had in common. He was part of the Disciples of the Road motorcycle club and I'd admit to being nervous upon meeting him for the first time. But he was only rough around the edges, with a soft center, and we continued to remain in regular contact.

"I have a favor to ask," Cassie said, biting her lip.

When she got that look in her eye it meant something important. "Lay it on me."

She heaved one of the couch's throw pillows onto her lap. "We've got summer break coming up."

"Right." I took a hearty sip of my wine. I had a feeling I was going to need it.

"Have you decided if you're going home in June?" Her eyes darted to the wall calendar we kept in the kitchen to keep track of our overlapping schedules.

"My parents won't be around. They're taking some cruise," I said. "Besides, I've got to put in lab hours and prep for my final class in July."

"My cousin's getting married at Shady Pines," she said, letting more of her Southern twang slip through.

Cassie had grown up in the small town of Roscoe. Shady Pines was the name of her family's game preserve. Guess the property was large enough to host a family wedding.

"Is this some big shindig with moonshine and kissing

cousins?" I was more than curious about her upbringing, having only heard random stories here and there.

"Very funny," she said, her lip twisting into a reluctant grin. "This might be the way to squash those crazy ideas in your head once and for all."

"What do you mean?" She'd been trying to convince me of the preserve's charm and apparently pictures didn't do it justice.

"I wondered if you'd be my date." Her gaze was deadly serious.

"Date?" I nearly choked on my wine. "What's the catch?"

"If I bring somebody, they'll lay off how '*right*' Jerry and I are for each other," she said, using air quotes. "My father has been persistent—even Grammy can't rein him in."

"Jerry?" I scrunched up my nose. "Why is this the first time I'm hearing about this guy?"

She threw her arm dramatically across her forehead. "Because I rarely think about him unless I need to visit my family."

My eyebrow quirked. "They're trying to set you two up?"

"Been trying for years," she said, her hands turning into fists. "His family's property aligns with ours and our businesses intersect at times. They have some insane notion that if we finally got back together, we could expand."

"Holy shit, it's like that reality show—Swamp something or another—but Florida style," I said. "So I take it you're not very fond of Jerry?"

"Can barely stand him anymore," she said. "We tried dating once and it was decent for awhile. He's handsome but also has traditional ideals about men and women. Believe me, I have enough alpha males in my own family."

The thought of all of that testosterone might fuel my imagination for several months. But it also explained why Cassie dated plenty of brainy geeks in this campus town, the type of guy who was in direct contrast to the men she'd grown up with.

And showing up with me? It was as if she was intentionally trying to prove a point.

"You do realize I'm gay, right?" I asked and she chuckled. "Your family doesn't know your roommate likes boys?"

"No, I never mentioned that." She cringed. "Actually I never even mentioned that you were a guy at all."

My mouth fell open. "Are you for real right now?"

Thinking back, I couldn't remember a time I'd even heard her recite my name in the brief phone calls with her father or grandmother.

"This is a completely different way of life," she said, motioning to our apartment and probably the city of Raleigh in general. "My move to a different state was enough of a shocker for them."

I sighed and reached for my reading glasses on the table. I only needed them for the smaller print on my phone, which was pretty much always. I noticed a new text from my friend about some hot guy he met at our favorite gay club in the triangle area.

"Let me guess," Cassie said. "Tate?"

"Begging me to come up to The Nickel," I said, typing back that I was in for the night. "I can't imagine what your family would think of our flamboyant friend."

"My dad might have a panic attack. He's always stressed as it is." She shook her head grimly and balanced her slippers on the edge of the coffee table.

"Especially if Tate wore one of his screen-print designs. The pink one with the rhinestone tiara," I said, suddenly thankful that Tate lived in this fairly diverse town, amongst friends who accepted him.

"So you can pretend, right?" Cassie asked, steering me back to her original request.

"To like you?" I asked. "I already adore you...but not in that way."

She rolled her eyes. "Just hold my hand and kiss my cheek every now and again."

"Suppose I can do that." I imagined all those times as a kid, wishing I could be *normal*. Acting like it for a long while. And now I was being asked to fake it again. Piece of cake.

"The townsfolk will be swooning over you," Cassie said, reaching over and running her fingers through my coarse black hair. She always said she had thick hair envy, even though her finer auburn locks were gorgeous. "Even I can admit you've got amazing sex appeal."

I scrunched up my face. "Not sure I get it."

"Fresh meat," she said and I wanted to point out that there was plenty of hunky flesh in her brothers. And on the preserve. I nearly felt faint. What the hell was I thinking agreeing to spend time with people who hunted animals?

"Plus, you can see the pretty countryside," she said, still attempting to convince me of her inane idea. "We'll show you around."

"You mean there are other things to do besides shooting wild boars?" I failed to mention how petrified I was of any kind of swine after one nipped me on a family trip to a farm. Even having it served at the dinner table didn't give me the satisfaction, only made me want to puke.

Cassie grinned. "I hope your misconceptions are blown through the roof, my friend."

"Will there be any vegetarian options?" I asked, thinking about my mostly raw-food diet. The thought of any kind of wild meat left me practically dry heaving. "You know me and my high-maintenance eating habits."

"We have a large garden and Grammy's a great cook," she said. "By the end of the week, you'll never want store-bought produce again."

"If I didn't know any better, I'd say there was a hint of

nostalgia in those eyes," I said, smirking. "I think Backwoods Betty is glad to be going home."

"I guess I can hate on my family all I want until someone from the outside tries to mess with them," she said, and I thought of how my younger brother and I would fight tooth and nail as kids. "Besides, I miss Billie. Callum, too."

How could anybody forget Cassie's hot ginger brother from those photos?

"So you'll do it?" she asked, pouting for effect.

I stood up and stretched before heading to the window to check on my vast assortment of herbs and potted plants. I pulled off a couple of dead brown leaves, as I thought her idea through.

I supposed I could beg Tate to keep my indoor garden watered while I was gone.

"Not sure I can handle a whole week, Cassie."

"How about we drive your car down for the trip?" she said, looking earnest. "Then you're free to ride back straight after the wedding. I plan on staying longer. Deal?"

It would be nice to get away from the city. I happened to enjoy wide-open spaces, along with some peace and quiet. Though I wasn't sure how quiet it would be on a game preserve.

"Does this mean I can ask you to one of my family's boring events in the future?"

My parents chose to ignore the topic of my being gay whenever it came up. Having Cassie around for some comic relief would be like a breath of fresh air.

"Of course," she said around a yawn.

A devious grin graced my lips. "When do we leave?"

2

CALLUM

I adjusted my grip on the pole. "I've got this one, Grammy."

"I trust you do, Callum," she said, yanking the ball cap over her eyes to blot out the blazing sun. "You always make me proud."

I'd give anything to be wearing my beat-up sneakers right about then, except you didn't mess with rattlers. Rubber boots it was. But they didn't scare me. Been doing this practically my whole life and only been bit once, by a black racer—a rattler's worst enemy.

My finger traced over the scar on my thumb as I dangled the noose toward the rattlesnake hole, waiting on him to surface. The dead mouse lay on its side, a decent last meal.

Hunters needed to keep a brave front, even if their knees were quaking. That's what Grammy always said when we were kids and she was one of the gutsiest people I'd ever known. She could probably still take down a wild boar with one perfectly timed shot. But her knowledge of gators impressed me most of all. She said the key was to respect their raw power.

One neighbor had his arm taken off at the elbow because of a ridiculous bet during the height of alligator season. You couldn't be reckless in this business, not if you wanted to succeed. The money we earned from avid and responsible hunting kept our preserve thriving.

A blur of white—probably one of the folks visiting today—flashed in my side view, making me lose focus for one nanosecond. But that was all it took, because now I was eye to eye with the snake, and he was a beauty. Brown markings trailed down his center while his striped tail rattled off the signs of trouble.

"Isn't there some law about killing snakes in this state?" I heard our company say. Even out of the corner of my eye I could see that the guy was one of them pretty city boys. He was walking beside my sister, Cassie, who was busy filling him in on rattler containment on personal property. He must've been the guest she'd mentioned bringing.

Did he need to be that handsome? Too bad he had to go and open his mouth.

"We can always walk away," I said. I didn't dare take my eye off the rattlesnake for a second time. "But that leaves you out here with no protection."

I heard him gulp at the same time Grammy snickered. "Sounds like our Cassie might've brought home some tree hugger."

Grammy gripped the heavy rock in her fingers, ready to bash the rattler's skull at a moment's notice.

"They say when a rattler strikes, your blood turns to fire. Like the venom is boiling away in your veins," I said and I could hear whatshisname's breathing change. "You've got about a ninety-minute window of time before the poison spreads."

"And then what happens?" he asked, and I could just imagine his pulse throbbing in his neck. I heard his one foot scrape across the other as if rubbing some imaginary dirt from his spotless shoes. Either that or it was some nervous tick.

I shrugged. "Then you're dead."

"Knock it off," Cassie said and I could hear the tightness in her voice. It pained me that we hadn't been in touch for a long while and I certainly didn't want to piss her off even further.

The snake retreated toward its hiding spot and disappeared without a second glance at the mouse. *Damn.*

Now I looked our new guest square in the face while my irritation bubbled over. Grammy had banked on making a fresh batch today. Lately I left the hunting to my brother Braden, but he had a full plate, so I agreed to be a stand-in. "You Cassie's date for the wedding?"

"That's right. I, uh, attend the same college," he said and I couldn't help my gaze from snagging on the deepest set of blue eyes. Not quite as dark as that tangle of hair that swept in a high arc away from his forehead. Wearing a pair of fancy designer jeans that showed off his trim form, he was smaller than me, but most guys were. And now I felt shitty for checking out my sister's guest. "The name's Dean Abbott."

"I'm Cassie's brother Callum. This is our grandmother, Sibly Montgomery," I said and he visibly swallowed, probably because of my tone of voice. "I'd say I was pleased to meet you, if you didn't make our rattler skedaddle."

"Huh?" he said, scratching his head. "Isn't that a good thing? You didn't want me to frighten him away?"

"We were set to make more rattler jerky," Grammy said and I watched Dean pale while my sister's lips drew in a tight line. Guess she never told him all the ins and outs of our family business. Probably a good thing or he might not have agreed to come. "We don't believe in gassing out these reptiles like other farms do."

"It's a more humane way," Cassie mumbled and the look of stunned silence on Dean's face said it all. He didn't believe in a lick of it.

"We respect the animals in the wild," Grammy said. "They live in their natural habitats and we mostly leave them be, unless it's a matter of survival or livelihood."

"Save your breath, Grammy, we've got nothing to hide," I said, gripping the pole until my knuckles turned white. Dean's eyes fixed on me like I was some kind of backcountry savage and I didn't like it. Not one damn bit.

"I believe you," Dean said in a sharp voice. Oh, he was going to be a lively one. Usually the guys Cassie brought home were pansies. "You run a respectable business. One of the largest in this part of the state. At least that's what Cassie said."

And then he awkwardly reached out to grasp her hand as if he only just remembered he was her date. "My degree is in biology. I look forward to hearing more about your industry."

I narrowly avoided rolling my eyes. Bet he'd rather chalk up the violations with the humane society. Except we ran a clean business. Something we took pride in.

All at once I heard the faint rattle in my ear. The snake had emerged from his hole and positioned himself between the mouse and Dean. Shit. We needed to act fast.

Dean had frozen in place, his mouth shaped in a perfect circle.

"Don't move," Cassie mumbled.

"I have half a mind to leave you hanging there, see where your fancy degree gets you," I said.

"I never...that wouldn't be cool," Dean ground out, his voice shaking.

"He wouldn't dare." Cassie threw me a death glare and I knew I had crossed the line.

I stepped to the side and nudged Dean out of the way. He lost his footing and ended up in the dirt. In one swift lunge I captured the snake's head in my noose. His body swung wildly in circles attempting to break free.

"Fuck," Dean said from ground level. Then he skittered back crab-like reminding me of gym class exercises.

Grammy bashed the rattler to the ground with her rock right before whipping out her knife and chopping off his head.

"Bag 'im up, Callum." She threw a smug look at Dean before turning toward the house. "Cassie, come have a nice chat with your grandmother. Callum will steer your guest back home."

Cassie bit her lip and threw a glance at Dean while I scooped the snake carcass into a sack. "You okay if I walk back with my grammy?"

Dean nodded even though it looked like he wanted to crawl on her back like a monkey and never let go. He watched as they walked away, Grammy still gripping the knife in her hand. But not before Cassie glowered at me in warning to play nice.

"Just great," I heard Dean mutter as he picked himself up and dusted off his jeans. My eyes couldn't resist following the motion of his fingers over his lean hips. I'd always liked my guys fit and angular. Not that I had more than half a dozen to speak of over the years.

I looked down at those clean sneakers he wore with those white athletic socks. "Here, I'll teach you a trick if you're going to wander around out here."

Dean's head snapped up in surprise. He probably figured I was just fucking around with him.

"Clap your hands as you're walking," I said demonstrating for him. I used my whole palm as I smacked my hands together. "That usually scares rattlers back into their caves."

"Thanks," Dean said and shrugged. "I'll only be here for a few days before I have to get back to my job."

"Maybe so, but you can use it anywhere in the southern states —Georgia is teeming with timber rattlers."

"Uh, true." The way he said it, I got the impression that he never stepped foot out of his air-conditioned office. Maybe he also worked out in some cushy gym given his solid thigh muscles in all that tight denim.

I trudged past the steep incline with purple and yellow wildflowers scattered along the crest.

"These are Cassie's favorite." I motioned over my shoulder. "You might want to pick some for her. Just a suggestion."

He walked a few steps up the rise and bent down to group a bunch in his hand. The dude had better treat my sister right. He didn't know who he was dealing with. I sure as hell never wanted Cassie to wind up with that knucklehead Jerry, but at least Jerry paid attention to what she liked.

Dean looked at the flowers he'd gathered and his eyes softened around the edges. I wondered who or what he'd just been thinking about. Better have been Cassie.

"Guess you're pretty good with the romantic gestures," he mumbled.

I grunted. Little did he know, if I had somebody to show that side to, I could be all about romance. But that idea would never come to fruition and lately all I could think about was screwing, because it had been weeks. No one in my family even suspected I was gay. At least I didn't think so, though I wondered about Billie sometimes.

My father would probably have a coronary on the spot if I told him. But it was Grammy's respect that I was most worried about losing. After my mother passed, her love was the closest I felt to that similar kind of affection and acceptance. I had a feeling she'd understand, but I was terrified to ever let it slip and be mistaken.

"I'm just showing you the country way of doing things," I said. "In case Cassie never told you much else about us or how we live."

"I've seen pictures of you," Dean said, trailing behind me.

"Huh?" I asked, turning back to glance at him. I was helplessly drawn to his thick eyelashes and pouty lips. "On Cassie's phone and your family's website."

"Oh, right," I said. "I thought we should establish a homepage and get with the twenty-first century. My brother Braden figured we should pose for it."

"You, um, look better in person," he stammered as a line of heat climbed up his cheeks. "I mean, because..."

He obviously wasn't flirting with me, but he was definitely poking fun at me. Sure, we looked like the damn Dukes of Hazzard or something on our webpage, but that didn't give him the right to amuse himself, not for his own benefit.

"You're not the first guy Cassie's brought home thinking he's got some superior education," I said, gritting my teeth. "And you won't be the last."

"That's not at all what I..." His hand flew to his chest. He looked stricken. City boy needed to learn better manners. And quick. "I didn't mean it like that."

Yeah, right. I stormed toward the house that was now in plain view and after another minute realized that he wasn't even following me.

I was sure I had overreacted, but damn it, how dare he show up here looking all hot and good enough to eat?

3
_____

DEAN

What in the hell had just happened? We'd only arrived and I had already pissed off Cassie's brother Callum. But honestly, he was being an asshole. Just digging for something to be angry about and apparently I was his target.

I found my way down the long trail to the main house, refusing to follow behind Callum, like he was some messiah leading me out of the desert. Though I was nervous about seeing another rattlesnake, I think he was more than likely just messing with me. It wasn't like the property was teeming with them. If so, why would they have been so disappointed to have missed the opportunity with just the one?

Cassie sat in the wooden swing on the large wraparound porch with her grandmother. She met my gaze just as I caught the tail end of Callum—and what a fine tail it was—as he went grumbling past her inside the house.

Her furrowed brow expressed an apology and I felt ridiculous that any of that had even happened. I gave her a small headshake, not wanting her to feel bad, and then handed her the bouquet of wildflowers.

"These are my favorite. How did you...?" Her jaw dropped open in surprise. I heard more grumbling from inside the house, and her grandmother turned away as a smirk lined her lips. "Thank you."

Sinking down on the wooden steps below them, I caught my breath. I looked out at the property, finally able to appreciate it, without worrying about any wild critters or brooding brothers. It looked vast and green with towering pine trees that stretched for miles, like toy soldiers in formation, as they ate up the sky, hills, and valleys.

"It would be great to go for a run," I said, already missing my jogging and biking routes in the city. But here in the wide-open space with the wind at my back would feel glorious. "Are there more trails?"

"There are," Cassie said, eyeing me doubtfully. How bad could it be? Would I smack into a boar or gator? "You should probably take the week off."

My eyebrows darted upward. "Why? It would be perfect out here."

Grammy chuckled and sank back in the swing. "Well, it's good to know you do more than study up there at that fancy university."

Just then the screen door slapped open and a lanky teenager with medium brown hair painstakingly made his way across the wooden slats carrying a tray of drinks, while a golden Labrador retriever closed in on his heels.

"There you are, Billie," Grammy said. "Offer our guest some of your sweet tea."

"Would you like some?" The kid, who was obviously Cassie's younger brother if his eyes and nose had anything to say about it, looked a bit breathless and fragile. I almost stood up to help take off the load but had a feeling that would not be a good idea—to Billie or anybody else. That's when I saw a silver medical bracelet dangling off of his wrist.

If I squinted, I might've been able to read the writing that had been inscribed on it, but that would've been rude.

I didn't want to admit I had never in fact liked sweet tea. Therefore I took the glass gratefully, so that Billie could finally place the tray down on the side table.

"This is refreshing, thank you," I said, after sipping out of my glass. It was some of the best tea I'd ever tasted, actually. Not too strong or sugary, just right. "I'm Dean, by the way."

"I'm Billie," he said, beaming, maybe because I complimented his batch of tea. Right then, I noticed something different about him that didn't come across on the photos I'd seen on Cassie's phone. Something in his eyes that told me he'd been through a lot and was probably an old soul. "Are you Cassie's b...boyfriend?"

I nearly choked on my tea. Thankfully Cassie saved me. "Billie, he's...he's my date to the wedding. That's all for right now."

Cassie shot me a look that told me to keep my trap closed, so I simply nodded.

"So tell me what you do, Dean," Grammy said and I felt my face grow hot like I was on the witness stand or something.

I heard some clanging from the kitchen and could just make out Callum busying himself with something, the likes of which I didn't know. Hopefully he wasn't skinning that rattler right at the damn table. Every now and then his gaze would swing to mine through the screen door. He was so damn good looking I couldn't help but blush. He was as large as a mountain lion with a mane of chestnut hair to match. I felt scrawny in comparison.

But I assumed that tough guy act back on the trail was Callum trying to figure out whether or not I was treating his sister right. I needed to get my shit together and show this family that I was worth something. Really, that Cassie was worth something to me. That wouldn't be hard because I adored her.

"I'm a research assistant at the university," I said in Grammy's direction. "We're studying the structural and mechanistic basis of signaling in insect odorant receptors."

Grammy just stared at me and Cassie nodded her head in approval. There was a smirk from somewhere inside and I tightened my jaw.

"Bugs have odor thingies?" Billie asked, his voice full of wonder.

"Yep, they use them to mate or to ward off danger from predators," I said, setting my tea down.

"Whoa," Billie said in awe.

"Bet you guys have interesting creatures out here," I said, hoping I didn't just jinx myself and some killer bees were on their way from the trail to sting the shit out of me.

What the hell was I going on about? I knew my insects and the only kind we didn't see as regularly in the southeast would be fire ants, palmetto bugs, and maybe some black widow or brown recluse spiders.

"Looks like you got yourself a smart one here, Cassie," Grammy said and my eyes sprang to hers questioning whether or not she was making fun of me. But this time she had a genuine smile planted on her face and I released the breath I was holding.

"I don't hold a candle to Cassie," I said, and her eyes softened. "She works for a professor, always has a lot on her plate, and is generally amazing."

There was a glint in Grammy's eyes so I think I hit pay dirt. Maybe they wondered what Cassie was up to all this time and hearing it from somebody who saw her regularly in her other life was something they appreciated.

"Your property is really nice," I said, breathing in the warm and fresh breeze. It was definitely different than city air, which could smell like fuel, metal or smoke depending on the day.

In the distance I spotted an extended structure along the west side of the property and wondered if another family might've lived there. "What is that cabin used for?"

"Visitors. Every year the neighbors next door have an alligator harvesting program and we have open season for deer and quail, depending on the month," Billie said, seeming to break it down in simple terms for me, as if I were naive or something. And possibly when it came to this topic, I was. Or maybe it was just how Billie communicated, guileless and to the point. "You have to have a valid license and folks reserve our cabin overnight."

"So groups stay out here to hunt on your land or the property next door?" I asked.

"That's right," Grammy said. "Quail, deer, wild boar, gators, pheasant. The law in most states is very specific. You're only allowed to tag a certain number of animals and then you're done. It also keeps certain wildlife from overpopulating."

"Tag?" I asked and felt a chill up my spine when I noticed in my side view Callum's presence behind the screen door listening to our conversation.

"*Hunt*," Billie said. "You can't go crazy, you only have a certain number you can track and shoot for dead."

I had never really given hunting much thought, despite my vegetarian status. I realized now how shitty it was of me to assume I knew what the hell my principles were on this sort of thing.

"The Lorrigan family lives next door. *Jerry,* his sister, and his mom and dad," Cassie spoke up all of a sudden, trying to help me understand, and I was beginning to get a decent picture now. So if Cassie were to hook up with Jerry again, even marry him, the two families could maybe expand or merge their property. What a lot to hang on Cassie. No wonder she felt like escaping.

"They have a gator preserve," she said. "It gets crowded over there, especially during the months of August and September, so we offer accommodations to their guests when they need it."

"What about the rest of the year?" I asked, genuinely curious now.

"Our cabin is pretty booked several weeks in advance for

general hunting. But there are other expeditions the boys are involved in like shrimp and crawfish harvesting," Grammy said.

This was such a completely different way of life I couldn't even wrap my brain around it. I grew things in a lab under artificial light and this family was living off the land.

"You do all of that hunting too?" I asked Billie and his face fell. Right away I knew I had asked the wrong thing and I wanted to kick myself. But a loud motor saved me because right then a couple of four-wheelers pulled up from a path behind the house.

Cassie stood up with a huge smile on her face, waving. "Daddy."

Mr. Montgomery parked and climbed off the vehicle. He was a large man, much like Callum. The other guy, who must've been their brother Braden, was leaner with light brown hair, but still, the family resemblance was unmistakable.

Suddenly my hands felt clammy. If Callum didn't like me, would the other men in the family follow suit? I might've just put my foot in my mouth with Billie as well.

I stood waiting while Cassie hugged her father and brother. The screen door slapped open and I could feel Callum's presence behind me. As well as his heat.

"Relax, son," Grammy said to me from the swing. "You're wound tighter than a music box."

I heard Callum smirk and as he moved past, his shoulder rubbed against my arm and warmth crawled across my cheeks.

"Everything look okay out there?" he asked his brother and father.

"Fine," Braden said and then his gaze swung over his shoulder. "Who's this?"

Callum looked back at me. "That's—"

Before he could get the words out Cassie cut him off. "He's my date to the wedding and also a friend. Dean, meet my father and my brother Braden."

Callum watched me as I stepped forward to shake his brother's hand. When I turned to Mr. Montgomery, there was something unyielding in his gaze. Guess he really did want his daughter to end up with Jerry. Or he was as protective as Callum. I didn't get that sense from Braden though, not yet. Damn, who knew this was going to be so awkward?

"Your cousin arrives in a couple of days for wedding prep to begin," Mr. Montgomery said to Cassie.

"I'll help any way I can," she said with a smile and her father threw a giant arm around her shoulders. I could see the affection for his daughter in his eyes.

The group moved toward the porch.

"Lunch?" Mr. Montgomery said to Grammy.

"Billie and I prepared some soup and sandwiches," she said, rising from the swing and depositing her empty glass of tea on the tray. Billie kept his hand on the back of the yellow lab, as if to steady himself. And now that I thought about it, the Labrador had never moved from his side on the porch. Was he a therapy dog?

"Good, I'm hungry," Braden said. "I could eat an entire gator."

Billie snickered as I tried to control my gag reflex. "Hunting humor."

Cassie moved beside me and then held back as her family was fielding through the door. "I'm sorry. I should've only had you come down for the wedding day. My family isn't usually this—"

"It'll be fine," I said, breathing out. "It's beautiful here. Nice change of pace."

Her eyes scanned the horizon and her shoulders seemed to relax. I did not want to ruin this week for her.

"Seems like your family misses you and only wants what's best," I said in a soothing tone.

She met my gaze with a bit of trepidation.

"Thanks for being here for me." Then she laced our fingers together and we headed inside the house.

4

CALLUM

After chopping more wood, I got busy with paperwork in the home office the rest of the afternoon, while I listened to a ball game on a national station. I secured payment for the groups using our shooting range and wobble deck for target practice the next couple of weeks.

This task always fell to me and I was cool with it, because the idea of Braden or Dad trying to balance the books was laughable. They were much better suited overseeing the land, which required plenty of maintenance to keep it operational.

I also made sure we had our supplies stocked tight with hunting gear—mostly bright orange or camouflage—as well as bullets, knives, hats, gloves, and flags. We'd be ready to take the overflow from deer and gator season coming up, no question.

Most of our revenue came from two to three key months a year, but shrimping augmented our business as well. Dad was always nervous about ruffling the feathers of the Lorrigan family next door since their surplus supplemented our income. He had leaned on Cassie for a couple of years, asking her to play nice, all to please Jerry and his parents. No wonder she decided to move away to college.

I didn't subscribe to my father's insistence that Cassie give Jerry a second chance. You couldn't force a relationship. Sure, they seemed well suited years ago. But appearances could be deceiving and nobody but those two could speak to what happened between them. Maybe they were simply too young to think about family legacies back then.

Before I knew it Grammy was clanging the dinner bell. I removed my favorite worn New York ball cap and hung it on the doorknob before Grammy gave me the third degree about wearing it at the table.

When I walked into the kitchen, Cassie was already seated beside Dean. I tried to keep my gaze from guiltily roaming all over the man who was here with my sister, from his dark hair to his midnight eyes that immediately sought mine out.

I had given the dude a hard time for no good reason. He was simply a date for the wedding and they might've only begun seeing each other. I wasn't sure why I was being such an ass and I probably needed to apologize for my earlier behavior. But for some reason, the guy got me all wound up.

I sat down directly across from Cassie. Billie and Dean were involved in a conversation about outer space, which Billie knew more about than anything else. It was one of his favorite topics, along with bird watching, and devising new recipes with Grammy. He was a cool kid all the way around. Smart as a whip too.

"Yeah, but the New Horizons space ship made it all the way to Pluto," Billie was saying. "So I bet they'll decide that it should be a planet again."

"I don't know," Dean said. "It's not like that decision was made lightning quick. It took them years to reach that conclusion."

"But now that they have photographic evidence from the actual..."

"Time to cut it off, " my dad said in a stern voice. "No space talk during dinner."

Daddy loved Billie to bits but always had a low tolerance for the things he felt so passionately about. Billie was born with epilepsy and Mom had died shortly thereafter, so Grammy had a large hand in raising him. I always wondered if Dad held some resentment toward Billie for Mom hemorrhaging to death after giving birth to him.

It was an irrational thought and my dad would never admit to it, nor give Billie a hard time, but he had a broken heart for years afterward. Still, he provided the best medical care for Billie and had agreed to a therapy dog to save his life in case of a debilitating seizure in the middle of the night.

Billie looked sullen and Dean's lips had drawn tight, seeming to feel guilty for contributing to the conversation. I shifted in my seat and winked at Billie, while his dog, Bullseye, sniffed at his feet beneath the table, completely in tune with the change in mood. That animal had been one of the best additions to this family.

"So how long have you two been seeing each other?" Braden suddenly asked, probably in an effort to change the subject.

Dean startled at the question and looked over at Cassie, who worried her lip between her teeth.

"Um, not long...a few weeks." She grasped for Dean's hand and he held her fingers awkwardly. What the hell was that about? Was she way more into him than I assumed?

But then he leaned over and kissed her cheek. The way his full lips brushed across her skin made the blood rush straight to my dick.

I was either a fucking loser or it had been way too long since I'd gotten laid. I needed to call Jason for a one-nighter in Gainesville or download that app to hook up with local men. The one I was terrified somebody would spot on my phone. I'd only used it a couple of times and then deleted it straight after.

Throughout dinner we made small talk about our business and property. I noticed how Dean only ate the biscuits and green beans, never touching the baked hen Grammy had prepared. Christ, dude was probably a vegetarian to boot.

One big rule in these parts—you eat what you hunt. We didn't believe in shooting for sport. So whatever game was slayed that day would be on the dinner table that night or shortly thereafter. If it wasn't possible, then it was dropped off to the shelters around town to use in their soup kitchens.

That policy was made clear to our customers and I had half a mind to give Dean an earful as well, in case he was holding back for a different reason. But it wasn't my place. In fact, thinking about him this deeply wasn't either. I had no idea why the man was like a burr in my side and intrigued me at the same time.

We cleared the dishes from the table and Cassie helped pack up the leftovers while we headed outside where Braden and my dad were setting up a bonfire. I'd chopped enough fir lumber to last us to the end of the month and then some and I had my sore biceps to prove it. But pine smelled the best and seasoned the quickest. I made sure to leave the dense oak for the wedding reception later this week.

Dean sat down beside Billie on one of the wooden benches near the flames and I chose a seat across from them. As Billie whispered and pointed in the distance, I figured he resumed his discussion about the planets and galaxies from the dinner table, out of earshot of my father.

I couldn't resist admiring the lean line of Dean's neck as he gazed up in wonder at the sky. He seemed to be enjoying the dialogue as much as Billie and that made my chest feel funny. At least Billie had somebody new to share his interests with, even if Dean would be gone in another couple of days.

"Damn." Dean's Adam's apple bobbed as he swallowed, and I had to look away from all that smooth skin. "I'm not sure I've ever seen stars like this."

"Probably right, city boy." When he glared at me, my lips tilted into a smirk. Couldn't even help myself. There was something about pushing his buttons that got me fired up. Kept the mundane at bay. "Too much pollution where you come from."

His eyes fastened on mine and his jaw was set tight, as if he'd decided he wasn't going to allow me to egg him on. He simply nodded and went back to staring at the landscape and sky, seemingly in awe of everything around him, like he had never been in a forest setting or something.

We heard the sound of gravel as a black pickup drove up the long driveway toward the house. Cassie and Grammy stepped onto the porch carrying a cooler of drinks and watched as the truck parked in the turnaround.

"It's Mr. Lorrigan." Cassie stiffened beside our grandmother before she headed down the stairs to stand beside Dean and whisper to him about who our guest was, more than likely. She was probably relieved the entire Lorrigan family didn't show up.

Jeremiah Sr. climbed out of the cab, and his son Jerry's resemblance to him was uncanny. They were handsome men; I'd give them that. But Jerry was dumb as a box of rocks when it came to his business sense. Plenty of people had looks, but if you had no substance to back it up, it was a damn shame.

Maybe that was why his father was so eager for him to marry into a good family. He knew Cassie was sharp and seemed especially impressed when my father had announced that she'd be earning her master's degree in business out of state.

I noticed how Dean appraised Mr. Lorrigan as his arm slid possessively around Cassie. Finally the guy was showing some kind of emotional connection to my sister. If it happened to be protectiveness, then so be it. She looked up at him gratefully and stepped inside his embrace. Something about the action made me feel even stonier.

Mr. Lorrigan made nice around the circle as I grabbed the cooler from Grammy, placed it beside the bench on the ground, and reached for a cold one. He avoided direct eye contact with me as he always did, despite shaking my hand in a show of manners, before approaching Cassie.

"You're as pretty as ever," Mr. Lorrigan said, pulling her into an embrace. "The city been treating you well?"

She returned a rigid hug but smiled genuinely, maybe on the defensive about where his question was leading. Dean stood beside her, with his faded jeans falling perfectly across his hips, and his fitted T-shirt that I finally noticed read, Let Us All Pause For a Moment of Science. I snickered to myself and turned away to take a swig of my beer before he could notice.

As Cassie introduced Dean, I tried to imagine what the lean muscles looked like beneath his shirt. What else did I have to do besides kill myself with fantasies of my sister's new boyfriend? The five o'clock shadow already forming along his chin and the dark hair styled flawlessly above his ears was also mesmerizing.

And after lunch, when I saw him slip some black-framed reading glasses over his eyes, so he could see something Cassie had pointed out to him in the local newspaper, it had left me practically drooling. Apparently brainy men were sexy as hell.

Right then Dean's eyes darted up to mine and held. A pyrotechnics display fired off in my chest, leaving me a bit breathless. Could he tell that I'd just been checking him out and thinking about him naked? Or was he trying to gauge my reaction to our visitor?

When Mr. Lorrigan placed his hand on Cassie's shoulder, Dean kept his gaze centered on mine, but tightened his hold on her waist. Ah, so this show was to prove to me that he would protect my sister. Good play.

5

CALLUM

Mr. Lorrigan and my father went inside the house to discuss some business. Soon enough they ended up on the porch with Grammy and Braden, shooting the breeze about the upcoming festival in Roscoe, along with some town gossip about the owner of the Quail Inn hooking up with a waitress at the Sunnyside Up Diner.

Never a dull moment if you gave people something to talk about around here. Right about now, they were probably whispering about the new guy Cassie Montgomery had brought home for her cousin's wedding. I wondered if Dean's ears were buzzing.

I remained down by the fire with Billie, Cassie, and Dean, listening to all the peaceful noises that represented home to me —owls hooting and the crickets chirping. Dean would flinch every now and again when he heard a twig break, but I was so used to the sounds of the woods around us, that it nearly lulled me into a sleepy state. The more I stared at the fire, the more tired I became after such a busy day. I didn't know how Cassie and Dean were holding up after their long drive.

"I haven't seen a firefly in a long time," Dean said staring out at the pine trees where the insects were flickering their lights on and off for his entertainment. "They are the coolest things."

"Fireflies love standing water," I said, motioning to the creek and small pond we boasted on our property.

"You should do your odor study on them," Billie said in an excited voice that made Bullseye rise to a sitting position ready to pounce.

"Maybe I will." Dean laughed and then tentatively reached his hand out to Bullseye's snout to pet him. It seemed that Dean understood that the dog was more than a pet and up to this point, had respected the boundaries. Unless Billie had explained his condition to Dean while I was working this afternoon, he didn't seem to pry and I liked that about him.

"We used to catch them out here in Mason jars," Cassie said, a sense of nostalgia in her voice. "Poke holes in the top."

Dean shifted uncomfortably, his eyebrows scrunched. "Why did you do that?'

"Stupid kid stuff," she said, disentangling one of her legs from beneath the bench. "Remember, Billie?"

"It was to trap the bugs and study them," Billie said, stroking his hand across Bullseye's flank.

Cassie bumped her shoulder playfully against Dean's. "Don't go getting all philosophical on me. It's not the same as the zoo."

"What about the zoo?" I asked, and then cleared my throat, attempting to control my curiosity about the guy sitting across from me. But maybe if I found more to irritate me, it would throw a wet blanket on his appeal.

"Dean has a thing about the zoo," she said and he rolled his eyes. "He doesn't believe in them."

As her feet knocked against his sneakers, I noticed a casualness between the two of them, like they'd known each other longer. Had they been friends first?

"I just think those animals should be allowed to roam free in their own habitats."

"But for analysis—" Cassie began, but Dean cut her off as if they'd had this same argument before.

"Then it should be time limited. Their babies shouldn't be raised in captivity," Dean said in a persuasive tone. "Kids come to gawk and stare everyday. They have no escape. I think it's cruel."

I found myself wanting to know more. Here was a guy who had plenty of convictions. "Same with aquariums?" I asked, after taking a swig of my beer.

He studied me across the fire, as if waiting for me to bait him or say something cruel. I definitely regretted the way I had treated him earlier.

"Sure, same concept," he said, his voice weaker, almost defeated.

"I don't think Dean would want to stick around for gator season," Billie said, and Cassie nodded.

"The hunters around here use bang sticks and only under water," Billie said, lowering his voice, as if to keep this conversation away from Mr. Lorrigan's inquiring ears.

"Bang sticks—those are the long poles with a firearm attached to the end?" Dean said, looking a slight shade of green.

"It's the humane way," I said. "So the animal doesn't suffer."

I hadn't taken part in gator hunting for a few years now, leaving it up to Braden and my daddy to participate if they chose to. Though my dad was getting up in age and Braden enjoyed other aspects of hunting more. Regardless, I always stuck around our preserve to handle the excess visitors from the other property and any concerns they had about the use of the cabin. Shrimping was more my thing.

Dean didn't say anything for a long while and Cassie looked like she regretted bringing him here at all. Maybe it was too much for him—us country folks and our Neanderthal ways. I felt a well of frustration rise up.

"How is it any different than animals—or in your case, insects—being studied in a lab for science purposes?" I said and

Dean's head snapped up. His eyes remained fixed on mine, wary.

"The way I see it, we were placed here on this earth for a reason that maybe we don't understand yet," I said. "If we are to advance as a human race—to eat, seek shelter, live more comfortably—then we're going to use the resources we were given. Which means some of them get destroyed in the process."

"But there needs to be a threshold for those resources," he argued. "The rainforests, the jungles..."

I held up my hand. "I think we agree more than you're willing to admit. The idea is to treat whatever you touch humanely and with dignity. And that absolutely does not mean depleting it."

It grew quiet around the fire as Cassie and Billie watched Dean and me guardedly.

"You've got a point, Callum." Billie lay prone on the grass and stared up at the night sky. "How are we supposed to explore those other worlds in fancy spaceships if we don't use our resources to advance our knowledge?"

He looked so young and sincere lying there, as Bullseye adjusted his legs and lay down beside him, his nose resting in the crook of his arm.

Dean cracked a smile at Cassie and me and it was infectious. I couldn't help grinning back.

He leaned over to get a better view of Billie. "Do you by chance follow a physicist named Stephen Hawking?"

Billie sat up suddenly. "Shut up, he's amazing. One of his theories is that there are no boundaries in our universe."

"Still?" Cassie mouthed to me, because Billie had been following the scientist loyally for a couple of years now.

"Don't let Grammy hear you chattering away about him," I said around a smile. "You know Stephen Hawking doesn't believe in a supreme being."

"I guess he can be wrong about that one thing," Billie said as he plopped back down. "Except, I don't see why God would want

Daddy to feel so sad and lonely by making Momma die. Maybe he got his wires crossed by keeping me here and letting her go."

Dean shifted uncomfortably in his seat as if unsure whether he should be privy to such an intimate conversation. Cassie's watery eyes flashed to mine, sadness and regret present in them. Before she could speak up to comfort Billie like she was always so good at doing, I jumped in.

"Maybe God thought that you had something really special to offer," I said, my voice low and scratchy, as I sank down on the ground beside him. "And we wouldn't be able to appreciate your extraordinary gift unless he took her away to do some other job."

I could feel Dean and Cassie's gaze on me but I refused to look in their direction, keeping my eyes fixed on my baby brother, who'd had a tough road.

He sat up to listen to what I had to say and looked close to crumbling. Before I could even think to reach out to him first, he threw himself in my arms.

"Now you just sound like Grammy," he said real low.

"Maybe Grammy's taught me a thing or two," I said into his hair before I kissed the top of his head, his stray curls appearing dark as the night, close to the color of the gorgeous man sitting across from us now.

At this point all the fight had drained out of me and I just wanted to hit the hay.

"Maybe you learned some things too—about yourself—since Cassie went off to college." I heard my sister's quiet gasp at Billie's remark. I knew that she had struggled with her decision to get her master's in a completely different state, even though she hadn't shared any of it with me. And since she'd been away I had definitely stepped up as an emotional anchor for my younger brother.

I ruffled his hair and held his slight body away from mine. "Now don't go getting all sappy and thoughtful on me. I've had enough for one night."

He sat back with a grin before standing up and finding a mauled tennis ball on the ground for Bullseye to chew and chase in the yard. We sat in silence watching Billie and his loyal companion for a while longer, enjoying the flickering fire and the array of shimmering stars.

"I didn't come here to cause trouble, Callum," Dean said in a soft voice, his eyes pleading. My gaze snagged on his full lips and the sincerity in his features. "I'm Cassie's guest. I meant no disrespect."

"I apologize for the way I treated you earlier. I get that you have a problem with the way we live," I said, holding his gaze steady. "But you're on our property and I'd appreciate it if you keep your opinions to yourself when Daddy or Grammy are around. This business has been in our family for a hundred years and we're just trying to keep our heads afloat. There's as much to be said for tradition and hard work as there is for modernizing their views."

"Agreed," Dean said, his eyes flicking all around my face. "My intention was never to insult anybody."

"It's cool," I said. "Believe it or not, I respect your opinion as well. You're smart and kind to my sister, so I hope it works out for the both of you."

Cassie ducked her head and Dean looked away, muttering, "Thanks."

My stomach throbbed. I need to get over this ridiculous fascination with my sister's boyfriend. I finished the rest of my beer, but before I could get up and say good night, Dean beat me to the punch.

"I'm heading to bed," Dean said, leaning over and giving Cassie a peck on the cheek. "Going for a run in the morning. Billie told me about a good trail."

"Which one?" I looked down at Billie, who had taken a seat by the fire again.

"I told him he should head along the creek up to Pines Ledge," Billie said.

I nodded in agreement, because it was a pretty view and a straightforward path.

"I didn't realize you were so active," I said to Dean.

"Bikes everywhere in the city, too," Cassie said. "How would you know much of anything about Dean anyway? You only just met him a few hours ago."

I raised my eyebrow at my sister's snarky retort. Touché. She stared back unabashedly and I saw how Dean tucked a smirk in the side of his cheek.

"Running keeps me sane," Dean said with a glint in his eyes. Then he turned on his heel before I could say anything more. "Good night."

6

DEAN

This ranch featured six bedrooms, three on each side of the house, with one in-law suite off the great room, which was an addition for Grammy. I had been set up in a guest room next door to Billie and across the hall from Callum, whom, at the moment, I was relieved to get away from. He had challenged my judgment, reason, and sense all day long and my muscles were so twitchy, they ached. A run would be refreshing in the morning.

As I lay down on the firm mattress beneath the comfortable sheets, I continued thinking about Callum, who somehow made my entire body thrum with tension. I couldn't exactly disagree with his philosophy about life. It was well thought out and sound. Screw him for making me question everything I had believed I stood for.

And the way he looked at me, like he was unraveling me piece by piece? Damn. I couldn't help wondering what other assumptions he'd made about me.

The larger question was why did I even care? That was my final thought before I finally dozed off.

When the alarm on my phone woke me out of my sleep, I had

been dreaming of Callum saving me from being eaten by a crocodile. Seriously, the man was fucking with my brain.

Was I really doing this? Running on this unfamiliar property in the early morning dawn? Being here had gotten my head so twisted up I couldn't even trust my own instincts anymore.

That thought propelled me out of bed. I was going for a jog, plain and simple. I threw on some running shorts and a loose T-shirt and headed through the dark and silent house.

When I stepped on the porch as quietly as possible, the sun was just rising in the east and I'd admit, it took my breath away. It was cool this time of morning, which was a relief from the mugginess of the night before.

I was bending over in a deep stretch of my calf muscles when the screen door swung open. My head jerked behind me as Callum stepped onto the porch. Guess he got up early as well.

I was too tired to talk even though my pulse was now thudding, so I merely grunted in his direction. He sat on the steps below me to tie his sneakers. He didn't look my way, only out at the horizon. The sky splattered with orange and pink paint strokes, as the world awoke from its slumber. It was truly picturesque and only motivated me further.

Callum's shoulders were taut with tension and I pondered why being in my presence caused him so much stress. It made me wonder if I had surrounded myself with so many similar-minded friends back in the city that I had almost become insular.

When I first came out in high school in a New Jersey suburb, it was a lengthy battle to become who I was meant to be. By college, I had already made a life for myself by ignoring most of the negativity, so that I could focus on being happy. I probably hadn't had anybody challenge me in a long period of time, outside of my professors at the university.

It made me want to place my hands on Callum's skin and work out those kinks, show him that I could soothe as much as ruffle.

Callum stood up suddenly and began stretching as well. He bent at the waist to touch his toes and then went into a deep lunge, facing away from me. I saw how his calf muscles were rock hard and I had to wonder how much of that power was natural.

"What are you doing?" I asked, finally breaking the silence between us.

"Going with you for a run," he grumbled, as he stretched his neck muscles. "Figure it was the least I could do since I wasn't very welcoming yesterday."

"I don't need a babysitter." The words flew out before I could stop them.

I should've been grateful but all I could hear was the underlying sting in his voice. As if I was simply one of his daily chores.

"Of course not," he bit out. "But figured on your first day out you might want company in case you run into any problems."

A shiver raced through me. He was only trying to spook me. I was just about to tell him so when a whimper came from the direction of the screen door. Bullseye was nudging at the handle, asking to be let out. Callum turned the knob to set him free and he sniffed fleetingly at us before rushing down the stairs to do his business in the yard.

I figured this was a good time to get moving, while Callum was distracted with the dog.

"Do whatever you want," I mumbled as I took off toward the trail that Billie had pointed out to me after lunch yesterday.

Starting at a slow and steady pace, I attempted to get my feet acclimated to the terrain, which consisted of dirt, patches of grass, and small scattered stones. I was used to strictly concrete, so my calves might very well take a pounding out here.

I actually wasn't sure if Callum would follow, but then his feet stomping the dense ground gave him away. When he caught up to me, I kept my eyes on the path, as some brush scraped past my thighs. When I next heard panting behind me, I nearly jumped out of my skin until I realized that Bullseye had joined us.

I couldn't help staring at Callum's powerful thighs out of the corner of my eye as he kept up his stride. He was a beautiful sight with his red brown curls pulled back in a knot at the nape of his neck. Though I nearly matched him in height, he resembled a beefy lumberjack. If I dared mention it, he would probably punch me in the nuts.

Sweat was pouring down my back and had I been alone I would've yanked my shirt off by now. So why hadn't I? Who the fuck cared? I was certain that Callum had seen plenty of bare chests in his lifetime.

I wrenched the shirt from my shoulders and pushed it sloppily inside my shorts. I could feel his eyes on me, probably marveling at how puny I looked next to somebody like him. Still, I had nothing to prove.

But when he ripped off his T-shirt as well, I clenched my jaw to hold in my gasp. All of that tanned muscle on display. When I finally turned my head toward him his eyes met mine and held. I slid my gaze away but not before noticing his bulging pecs and the line of lighter hair that circled his areolas and ran down the center of his chest.

Fuck. He was trying to torture me. I stared straight ahead before I gave myself away.

The only sound was our labored breathing and the wind rustling through the leaves. Had I been alone I would've been able to appreciate the charm and beauty of the landscape. But with him right beside me, my breaths were expelling at a faster rate, leaving me more winded than I had anticipated. When we dodged beneath a canopy of tall pine trees, the air surrounding us turned cooler, bringing me needed relief.

It was almost unsettling back here with the light intermittently blotted out from the tall trunks and high branches all standing at attention like warriors. Billie had described that the path just beyond these trees became an incline. It apparently led up to an outcrop with a huge rock to sit and take a break if I needed to before heading back.

When Bullseye tore ahead of us into the brush it forced my thoughts back to Billie.

"The dog doesn't need to stay by your brother's side at all times?" I asked, breaking the silence. I hoped he didn't think my question was insensitive. It was more out of curiosity and concern than anything.

"Billie hasn't seized in months," Callum said, between heavy gusts of breaths and I felt guilty for making him talk. But I had intentionally kept a slower pace, unsure if he had run anytime recently. In my own way I was still catering to him, even though he hadn't been gracious to me at all yesterday. I had half a mind to speed up, but I wanted to have this conversation, especially if it centered on Billie.

"Bullseye has been able to warn Billie before a seizure happens, so that he can get to a safe location," he continued. "That dog has saved his life. If Bullseye's away from him, it's only for an hour here or there when he's awake. Billie's the one who let him out in the hall. He knows Bullseye loves being in the woods."

I was in awe of the animal and of Billie. Epilepsy couldn't be easy to live with and I felt terrible that Billie has had to struggle his whole life with a condition that was debilitating to so many. Cassie had only mentioned in passing that her mother had died in childbirth when she was about ten years old and that she had a younger brother that had an illness.

But I naively thought it was a one-time thing, not a constant battle. Who knew that Billie was such a brilliant and interesting kid? If anything, I was glad to have met him on this trip.

A head of us there was a clearing and as we ran up the incline, we decreased our speed, both of us gasping for air. Though Callum looked more spent, his face red and sweaty, and again I questioned when he'd last been for a run.

I spotted the ledge with a wooden railing and the large rock Billie had told me about. I slowed my stride and pulled my water bottle from the pack on my hip. I jogged in place as I looked around.

I had no idea if Callum would keep going or join me for a short break, but regardless, I knew my way back to the house now. If anything, Bullseye was sure to lead me on the right path, unless he followed Callum home instead.

Callum skidded to a halt beside me and hunched over at the waist to catch his breath. He straightened after another second, and looking out into the distance, pulled his own water bottle out.

He took a long chug and then pointed into the vast brush. "See that enclosed area near the marsh?"

I looked in the direction of his hand. I saw a thick fence that appeared to divide this property from the one next door. There was a change in scenery as well. Whereas this preserve was lush and green, the Lorrigans' was more swampy and brown.

"That's where they bring the gators," he said. "The guests can hunt them all they want, but if they tag out, their season is over."

I squinted, trying to imagine the alligators swimming in the murky water and I'd admit, the idea of it unnerved me.

"The state has checks and balances in place for hunters," he continued. "Both of our families donate a portion of our earnings to a wildlife fund and the remaining gators are free to roam in the wild."

I got the feeling that he was giving me a lecture of sorts, or attempting to convince me of something. "You don't have to prove anything to me."

"I wasn't trying to," he said, his eyes darting to mine and then to the pines again. "Just figured you might be curious about how it all operates. That one month feeds plenty of families in the profession, much like the crabbing business along the Eastern Seaboard. Though we catch an ample amount here as well."

"So what does your family have to do with the Lorrigans' place besides helping with overflow on the land?" I asked, since we were actually having a civil conversation.

"Dad and Mr. Lorrigan have talked about merging for years now," he said, with a tightened jaw and I had to wonder why the subject seemed to irk him so much. "To expand the land and business."

"How does Cassie figure into any of that?" I said. "I mean, she told me about Jerry."

He looked at me with narrowed eyes and then his shoulders seemed to sag. "Guess lots of folks around here can be set in their ways. Still got their notions about how things should be, as far as combining respectable families in marriage."

I didn't dare breathe a word, eating up everything he had to say, because his viewpoint was always interesting. "Though I suspect Mr. Lorrigan might just be holding out on us and his son marrying Cassie is an excuse to keep us at bay."

My head snapped back at that revelation. "What do you mean?"

"Never mind," he said quickly, shaking his head, and I got the impression he said more than he meant to.

We drank our water in silence, simply breathing the cool air next to each other. When I spotted a large barren field, I asked, "What's that patch of land over there?"

"It's a dead zone. We can't get anything to grow," he said, cringing. "We've been trying to resurrect a sugar cane field, like my family had a few decades ago when Grammy was young."

I nodded, rapt with attention. "How many acres you got here?"

"Almost a thousand," he said. "And that patch of land is the one we struggle with most. After a time, we just gave up and figured out some other things."

Just then, Bullseye came bursting through the trees, hot on the trail of something he was chasing, and I remembered we were in the wild, and there could've been anything out there. Had I been here alone, I wasn't sure I would've taken this long of a break.

Still, I was enjoying the scenery and the breeze. And the company, if I was being honest with myself.

"You don't have to wait for me," I said, finishing the last of my water. "You can head back anytime."

"I'm cool, just relax," he huffed out. "If I wanted to leave, I would."

I rolled my eyes and could feel his gaze searing into me.

"How often do you run in the city?" The Southern twang to his voice was more pronounced when he was irritated.

"Almost every morning," I said. "Cassie knows that I—"

What the fuck was I saying? I couldn't let on that we were roommates. God, this was getting stupid and fast. Why couldn't she just tell her brother we were pretending? Exactly why were they no longer close?

I was going to ask her for more details as soon as I returned to the house.

Callum was still staring, waiting for me to continue. "I was just going to say that Cassie knows how much I need to run. It relaxes me, keeps me in shape."

His eyes slid down my chest to my stomach. I wish I knew what the fuck he was thinking.

"Of course I'm not as built as you are—you obviously do a whole bunch of weight training," I said, motioning to his physique.

"Honestly, I don't do much outside of working on the land," he said, scraping his fingernails across his chest and my gaze couldn't resist following his hand over all of that golden skin.

The smattering of auburn hair that sat in small tufts in the center of his chest and then ran in a trail below his shorts was so sexy. I imagined being on my knees right then discovering what treasure lay beneath that waistband. Holy fuck.

I squeezed my eyes shut before my boner filled with more blood.

"Genetics, I guess," he said, in a throaty voice. When I opened my eyes, he was watching me. "And your physique is just fine, by the way."

We stared at each other for a long awkward moment as I got my breathing, as well as my cock, under control. It was time to end this little outing before he saw the desire plain as day in my eyes.

"I'm going to head back," I said and without warning, took off into the brush, my body too overheated as it was. I wanted to get back to the house and jump into a cool shower.

He trailed behind me at first and I wondered if his muscles had tightened up on him or if he was done with this excursion as well. Soon enough though, he was beside me, breathing evenly through his nose.

We ran in silence most of the way back. But I could tell there was something he was stewing on. He had this habit of fishing his bottom lip through his teeth when he was about to say something.

"Are you and my sister..." he asked suddenly.

"Getting serious?" I said, filling in the blank. He must've read into something I said back there.

He nodded and I saw him swallow roughly, as he waited on my answer.

"You're pretty protective, aren't you?" I smirked.

"Wouldn't you be?" he asked, side-eyeing me.

"Sure," I said, shrugging. "Believe it or not, Cassie is fierce and can handle herself."

"Even still," he said and I could picture how he might've been when they were kids. How Callum was probably defensive over his siblings after his mother passed.

"Don't worry so much," I said, attempting to reassure him. "All is well. If we don't work out she's an amazing girl and we'll always be friends. I'll keep a watch out."

His eyebrows lifted. "You're already banking on not working out?"

Fuck, I needed to stop putting my damn foot in my mouth.

"I'm saying I would never intentionally hurt her and vice versa," I said, trying to smooth over my earlier statement.

No goodbyes were said when we finally made it back, we simply headed in opposite directions.

CALLUM

It was plain stupid to have gone on that run with Dean. Not only because my muscles were protesting but also because now I liked him more, was even more attracted to him. His trim body was exactly the kind I preferred, and those full lips sipping from that water bottle nearly sent me to my knees.

I still didn't know whether he had good intentions toward my sister, but my intuition told me he probably did. Good news was that he'd be gone in a few days' time and I'd be left with my fantasies, my hand, and a lingering hard-on.

Today we had a last minute group of shooters at the gun range. They'd be finished by the afternoon because of prep time for the approaching wedding ceremony, but that extra money would help us sit tight this month. Daddy always worried too much about the years ahead, even though I reassured him that our family was sitting on a nice little nest egg.

But he figured some kind of emergency was bound to happen to put us in debt right quick. Grammy always said that his logic had completely changed since Mom had died and he could never shake the feeling that his world might be turned upside down again.

Braden was in charge of loading the targets and after I washed up, I headed over in the three-wheeler, since it was more stable on uneven terrain, to see if he needed additional help.

I ignored the rush of the shower from the direction of the guest bathroom as well as the steam escaping beneath the door, as Dean got ready for his day. I adjusted myself on the uncomfortable seat as I pictured his naked chest. The inky black hair surrounding his nipples that became taut as pencil erasers from the cool air at Pines Ledge. Imagining what the rest of him looked like wasn't going to help matters much.

Fuck, I needed to cut this shit out. But I couldn't help my illusions from running rampant when I noticed him checking me out. I knew it was only in a curious kind of way but damn if it didn't get my blood pumping.

I pulled up to the range just as a group of five men exited their trucks. Braden was greeting them and beginning his spiel about the target practice.

I sidled up behind the group to listen to my older brother, who was the consummate professional and was fantastic as the face of our family business. I was better suited and entirely more comfortable behind the scenes.

"We rent shotguns here, but if you brought your own," he said, nodding to the man who had his double barrel semi-automatic leaning against his leg, "that's cool."

I caught Braden's eye and he shook his head at me, telling me in his own way that he had the session under control. Still I stuck around and helped lead them to the range and got them each placed in their own slot. Protective eye gear and earplugs were distributed to help blot out noise.

Braden and I stepped to the side to allow everyone to regroup and aim at the individual targets. I suspected some of these men were hunters, like the man who had brought his own equipment, more than likely to keep his skills sharp. But the others might've tagged along as part of a male bonding trip, which seemed more likely to me. There was a lot of shouting and high-fives.

They rented the pen for an hour of time before switching to the wobble deck to shoot at clay targets. Afterward, we needed to hightail it over to the open field on the south end to help clear more brush for the ceremony.

My cousin had hired some low-rent wedding planner. The whole nine yards at a bargain price as Grammy called it, so essentially they were only using our property. But we were lending them chairs and tables and were instructed by our daddy to help if they needed anything moved or supplied.

"Is Jennifer staying out here for the wedding?" I asked Braden. Jennifer was the girl he'd been dating for the past year. She was a nice person, but if I was being honest, I didn't know if she was the one for him. We had all grown up together in Roscoe, everybody knew each other's business, and this was a relationship that arose after a trip to one of the only local bars.

"She'd like to," Braden said, not sounding as enthusiastic as he should about the woman he'd been spending his time with. She had been placing pressure on Braden to get engaged but he was resisting at every turn. He was a hard person to talk to about it however, shooting me down every time I'd tried bringing it up in the past. Not that I was much more forthcoming about my own dating prospects. It was in my senior year of high school that I finally admitted to myself that I was gay.

Everything had gone haywire when I was twelve years old. After my mom died, Grammy stepped up to the plate to help raise Billie. She'd been living on the property anyway and her son —my father—needed all the help he could get. He was distraught by the sudden death of my mother, though they were told it was a high-risk pregnancy—we all were. Losing your mother felt like losing your foothold in the world. Suddenly everything had turned dark and terrible and devastating, like somebody had vacuumed up the sun.

It wasn't until Billie had his first seizure as a toddler that we snapped out of the fog and realized that he needed services or we'd lose him, too.

Despite us rallying as a family around the care of Billie for a few years, I had retreated inside myself after realizing I had a mad crush on the star pitcher of my high school baseball team. I avoided the locker room when he was changing, terrified that I would pop a boner. Having to stare at his tight ass in those white baseball pants from the outfield was torture enough.

I had been dealing with all of these crazy hormones and feelings and I didn't know where to put them. I had even pulled away from Cassie, whom I was closest to growing up.

Years later, I still felt her confusion and hurt over it.

Truth was, I was terrified of coming out in this small, conservative township, and I was worried she wouldn't understand, so I isolated myself, losing her companionship in the process.

"How come you don't have a guest for this wedding?" Braden asked and I stiffened. He hadn't questioned me about my dating life in awhile. I pretended to see this girl occasionally when I headed into Gainesville, but it was really Jason, who met me sometimes for a quick hookup. "What about that girl Sheila?"

I waffled, grasping at straws and then came up with my standard answer. "She's busy."

He narrowed his eyes. "She's always busy."

"Whatever," I said, watching the group of men who probably all had wives waiting for them back home.

My first sexual experience in college was with Jason, and he taught me the ropes, so to speak, as I earned my associate degree in agriculture at the University of Florida. College opened up a few gay doors for me, but living where I did now just pushed me further back in the closet. Then Cassie had earned her bachelor's degree, working toward her master's next. She left me here to suffer silently and we had grown further apart with each passing year.

"At least I'm not stringing somebody along because I'm too chicken to say goodbye," I muttered, kicking at a stone on the ground.

"It's more complicated than that," Braden bit out and then sighed because he knew I was right. "She's a good girl. I like spending time with her."

"I get it," I said, bumping his shoulder. "As long as you're clear where this is going. Then she's free to walk away if she needs to."

The arrangement I had with Jason and any other guy over the years was no strings attached. Jason was out to his family and friends and has had boyfriends here and there, but he understood my situation. That I was next in line to run this family business, that we relied on this income, and that breaking my father's heart yet another time was not a decision that I could make lightly.

"Is that the 'arrangement' you have with Sheila?" he asked using air quotes.

I ignored his quip, but damn, telling him the truth was right on the tip of my tongue, because sometimes it was exhausting, hiding who you really were. "Yeah, man."

After my shower, I got dressed, not sure what the day would bring. I had agreed to come to this family wedding with Cassie and pretend to be her date, but who would've known how difficult it would prove to be? Or even guessed that I'd be so wildly attracted to her brother? He was as different from me as the sun to the moon, besides being straight and so not into me.

"Dean, can I talk to you?" Cassie asked on the other side of the bedroom door.

After I let her in, she walked around the room eyeing the dresser and knickknacks, maybe having forgotten what this room looked like. She brushed her fingers over the angel figurines all lined in a row and I imagined her mother showing them to her as a child. She had a photo of her mom back at our apartment and I knew how much Cassie had favored her.

"How was your run?" she asked me absently, her mind somewhere far off, tucked away in a memory.

"It was good," I said, licks of heat curling around my stomach remembering Callum's torso in all his sweaty glory. "Your brother joined me."

She turned abruptly to face me. "My bro—"

"Callum," I said. "He wanted to be sure I was safe...I guess."

There was a blend of emotions in her gaze. Pride and melancholy mixed together. When she sat down on the edge of my bed, still thinking about it, I decided now was the time to ask.

I placed my hands on her shoulders in a light massage, like I always did. "Why doesn't any of your family know this is just made up between us?"

"Because the general consensus is that I jumped ship and I've been trying real hard to show everybody that I'm doing just fine on my own. I don't need to marry somebody from back home," she said, rolling her neck. "Even if it disappoints my dad. He always said I had a restless spirit like my mom."

Cassie had never seemed restless to me, though she kept herself plenty busy. More so I saw her as outgoing and bubbly. Maybe living in a bigger city was what she needed after all.

"What about your grammy?" I asked, more than curious about the woman who helped raise them.

"She is the best kind of lady. But truth be told, she remains Switzerland around here. The way a grandmother should be, I suppose," she said. "She was always there to listen. But she knew how to keep neutral. Even on this Jerry thing. It was kind of infuriating. Mom would've put Dad in his place. Told him to back off."

I smiled, imagining an older version of Cassie, telling it like it is.

"Your siblings?" I asked, staying general, even though I really wanted to zero in on the one brother. "Somebody you can confide in?"

Her eyes took on this sad, faraway look. "Callum and I used to be real close."

I sat down on the bed next to her and reached for her hand. "What happened?"

"He closed himself off. It was the summer after his senior year of high school," she said in a sad voice. "He just...I don't know. Wasn't the same brother anymore. To me. He was always there for Billie though, no matter what."

I felt a pang in my chest remembering how Callum had talked to Billie last night at the fire. How sensitive and vulnerable he'd sounded soothing his brother's fears. I imagined what it would be like to be close to your sibling and then all of a sudden *not*.

It had happened in a physical sense with my brother, Shawn, who had died of leukemia. But that was altogether a different kind of pain. Maybe the same kind of ache that Callum was fearful of experiencing.

"Did something happen to Callum?" I asked, my heart beating out of my chest, wondering what would make somebody disappear inside of themself.

"Not that I could ever put my finger on," she said. "Unless it had to do with making a decision about helping run Shady Pines. Braden was already assisting Dad, but Callum seemed unsure at the time. Grammy would say he needed to sow his wild oats."

"And did he?" I said, laughing at the terminology, especially when she said it in her Southern twang. "Sow them?"

"I have no idea," she said, throwing her hands up as if perplexed. "I have never even seen Callum with a girl. Not like Braden. Callum would go into town sometimes—maybe he was seeing somebody, maybe not. But one thing was for sure, he never told anybody about it."

I pondered that a second. Callum sure as heck seemed reserved, but more like stuff was just bubbling at the surface for him. Like he could explode at a moment's notice, yet only allowed you small glimpses of everything he was holding inside.

"Anyway," she said, standing up. "Don't want to keep Grammy waiting. Meet you at the breakfast table."

I pushed a comb and some gel through my hair, trying to appear halfway decent—for whom, I wasn't sure anymore—and then sat down at the kitchen table to inhale the most amazing breakfast with my coffee.

"These have got to be the best pancakes ever," I said around a mouthful and Cassie grinned.

"Grammy is the best cook," she said, pouring more maple syrup on her stack.

Billie was eating his fill across the table from me but the other Montgomery men were nowhere to be found. They probably had a million things to do on this land and I was learning to appreciate exactly what the job entailed simply from twenty-four hours of being here.

"Want to go for a ride with me on some four-wheelers?" Billie asked after a nibble from a long strip of crispy bacon. I wondered if there was a hog farm somewhere around here as well. I found the thought didn't bother me as much this time around. Besides, no way to escape carnivores around mealtime, even in the city.

I looked to Cassie with raised eyebrows.

"Billie knows his way around this property like the back of his hand and he can ride the four-wheeler as long as somebody is nearby, in case..."

"In case I have a seizure," Billie said, wiping his mouth. It was the first time anybody had mentioned his illness out loud in front of me. They had years to get used to the idea, I'd only just found out, so I tried to keep my face neutral. "But Bullseye will be with me too. And he'll know ahead of time, if..."

"Bullseye can't help if you fall off the bike," Grammy said, pointing her spatula at him. "Dean here would be a dear to ride with you."

"I'd love to go," I said and Grammy threw me a wink before she flipped more pancakes in the scalding pan. I felt like I had just been awarded a gold star.

"Now don't get crazy swerving that bike along those back roads, Billie," Grammy warned as he hustled out the door,

Bullseye on his heels. Then she turned a critical eye on me. "You keep him in check, you hear?"

"Will do," I said, in a salute, and then kissed Cassie on the cheek before carrying my empty breakfast plate to the sink.

I met Billie near the garage entrance as he waited impatiently on his four-wheeler, adjusting the strap of a sturdy white helmet. A second vehicle caked with mud was parked alongside. I had only been on one of these all terrain vehicles once in my life, but remembering how to fire up the engine was simple enough.

When I got the motor humming, I nodded in Billie's direction. He rolled ahead of me, driving at a slower pace while Bullseye ran beside. I wasn't sure if his speed was for the dog's benefit or my own, but I appreciated being able to get my bearings and a good look at the property at the same time.

As we cruised up and down the trails, I realized it was a hell of a lot of fun to simply take in the scenery while the wind whipped at my back. It was kind of how I felt on my bike in the city, except it was all concrete and busy sidewalks that you had to navigate around. This was serene and leisurely and wide open. Plus, the camaraderie wasn't so bad, either.

As we drove by the large patch of land with the dead soil that I had seen from Pines Ledge that morning, I asked Billie to pull over.

"Callum said your family tried to plant sugar canes here?" I asked him as we sat idling side by side.

"That's right," he said and then launched into the history of the preserve. It was definitely interesting to hear it from his point of view. There was pride in his voice as well as a bit of awe.

Apparently his great grandfather and his four sons started in the cattle business but then bought this land and turned it into the preserve it had become today. Animals were hunted on this property for several decades in conjunction with county ordinances that got stricter over the years.

"Did you know that boars are not indigenous to Florida?"

Billie asked in an excited voice, as if he were delivering a history lesson, and in a way I could see him in a classroom doing just that.

"I didn't," I said, looking around the property as if one of them might come charging out at me.

"Nope. They just pass through sometimes because they like a pine woodland best, next to marshes of course," he said with a chuckle and I wondered if he could sense my fear as I squeezed the handlebars until my fingers were bloodless.

"Are they feral?" I asked in the calmest voice I could muster.

"Nah, they're mostly just like any other animal making use of the land," he said and I relaxed. "The feral ones you hear about probably have rabies."

"Rabies?" I nearly shot off in the ATV to get back to the safety of the house.

"You should see your face." A hearty laugh burst from Billie's throat. "You are definitely a city boy. We haven't seen a wild boar around here in ages."

I shook my head and snickered along with him. I climbed off the four-wheeler to get a closer look at the soil. I scooped a pile of the brittle dirt in my fingers.

"You guys have a lot of weeds," I said, noticing the amount of leaves protruding from the flat landscape in the field.

"Yeah," he said, bending down with me. "Callum said they were probably choking the sugar cane roots."

"You have to keep up with the growth," I said, crumbling the dirt in my fingers. "But it can be a demanding job."

Sugar canes were known to be pretty resilient, so to see this field completely barren was a wonder. I picked up one of the abandoned leaves and noticed a spiky, crooked pattern traveling down to the rib of the plant. Some bits of information from one of my insect entomology classes niggled in the back of my brain.

"What did your family use the sugar canes for?" I asked, also wondering what kind of fertilizer they had used. The best kind for these types of plants was supposed to come from poultry. I'd have to ask Callum or Grammy about it.

"To make syrup," Billie said wistfully. "It was called Montgomery's Sweet."

"Cool. Was it better than the syrup I just ate with my pancakes?" I asked.

Come to think of it, the bottle looked store bought, probably locally, but still delicious.

"That's what Grammy says," he said, patting the dirt from his knees, as he stood up. "People would place orders months in advance."

Bullseye nudged at Billie's hand and he gently slid his fingers through the hair behind his ears. Their relationship was pretty wondrous to witness, as if so in tune with one another.

"What is it that Bullseye does?" I asked, my eyes fixed on Billie's fingers as the dog's mouth drooped open and a lazy tongue lolled out. "To warn you of a seizure? If you don't mind my asking."

His eyes sprang up to meet mine and a small smile played across his lips. "He nuzzles my neck to wake me up. And then licks at my mouth. The trainer said it was to make sure I wasn't choking on saliva."

"I wonder if Bullseye even realizes how special he is," I said, my voice pitched in astonishment, as I watched Billie brush his coat for a second more. "But I have a feeling he probably does."

"Ready to ride some more?" Billie asked, his leg already slung over the seat. I wondered if he ever got this much time to explore on a regular basis with everybody so busy on the preserve. It made me happy that I could spend some time with him.

I climbed on the four-wheeler and we had just gotten back on the trail when shots rang out.

10

DEAN

I nearly drove off the side of the road. "What the hell was that?"

"My brothers are with a group of hunters that rented out the property this morning," he shouted over the din of the motor. "C'mon, I'll show you."

"Is it safe?" I asked, the pancakes from earlier sloshing around my belly.

"Of course," he said and veered down another trail to lead us toward the direction of the noise.

As we drove into the clearing, I spotted a large multileveled wooden structure. There was a group of hunters spread out along each tier, rifles hoisted on their shoulders. I had never seen anything like it. The men shot at something in the distance, their attention focused solely on the targets.

I pulled the ATV to a stop next to Billie and Bullseye. "It's called a wobble deck and it's popular in these parts for target practice."

I watched as something flew into the airspace and as a hunter took aim, the object fell to the ground with a thud. My heart was thumping hard in my chest, bile crawling up the back of my throat. No way I could sit around while animals were being killed right before my eyes. I might be a guest but that didn't mean I had to partake in anything I didn't want to.

"What are they shooting at?" I asked, my pulse spiking. In another second I was going to tell him I needed to get the hell out of here.

Billie shrugged. "Clay."

My head snapped toward the target. "Not quail?"

Billie's eyes narrowed. "That takes place in the forest, especially since quail nest on the ground, and you have to be wearing your hunter orange."

I felt my chest loosen. So they weren't offering up random animals for these men to take direct shots at. There were rules and proffered times. Even though Callum had said so, I still needed to see it with my own eyes. I was glad in that moment it was Billie who happened to be answering my questions and not one of the other brothers.

"Do you hunt quail?" I asked Billie as he watched the men whoop and holler over their baffling recreational activity.

"I have," he said, looking a little uncomfortable. "Daddy has taken me out a couple of times. But I didn't enjoy it."

I arched my eyebrow. "How come?"

"Guess I'm too much of a softie," he said, his lip curling upward. "Daddy says I'd rather make friends with the animals."

Damn, I liked this kid. He smiled ruefully as if he knew we'd be co-conspirators in that mindset.

"But I love shooting the clay," he said and then pointed at the machine that helped launch the targets into the air.

Billie's phone buzzed in his pocked and he fished out his cell. When he looked at the screen, a smile crept across his face. For the first time, I wondered about the social life of a fifteen year old who suffered from epilepsy and used a therapy dog to help stave off seizures.

In the city, it would be easy for him to head out the door to meet friends at a coffee shop or movie theatre. But out here, it might've felt isolating. Maybe a whole other online persona played out for a kid who was raised on a preserve in a small town. Or maybe again, I was making too many assumptions.

Now that my breathing was under control, I focused in on Callum and Braden standing behind the wobble deck, having a conversation. Callum gazed over at us several times and there was a hint of something that passed through his gaze.

If I didn't know any better I would've said it was interest. Definitely in what Billie and I were up to, but more than that—something that felt a lot like attraction. But that didn't fit Callum's reticence and his snappish frustration with me. I was probably reading too much into it just because the man was one hulking giant with sex appeal oozing out of his pores. Standing beside his brother who was also tall, Callum still dwarfed him. Maybe it wasn't his sheer size, but more like his aura. It held me captive every single time.

Except I kept thinking about what Cassie had shared with me. That she'd never seen Callum with a woman and that something had changed his senior year of high school. It all hedged too close to home in the back of my brain.

The hunting group had finished target practice and headed to their vehicles. Braden and Callum were talking to the man who probably organized all of it for his buddies and took turns shaking his hand. I wondered if he was a regular customer.

"Want to try it?" Billie's voice broke through my thoughts.

"What?" I asked, angling my head. "Shooting at clay targets?"

"Yep," he said. "If you're interested, Callum will let me do it, too."

He sounded so young right then and it made me wonder just how strict and overprotective his siblings were with him. Or at least Callum, since Billie appeared to look at him with stars in his eyes.

"I've never shot a gun in my life," I said and Billie's eyes widened. "But I guess I'd be curious to give it a try."

Where in the hell had that thought come from? Was I just doing this for Billie's sake? I had never once given the idea of holding a weapon any consideration. But everything I thought I knew or believed had been flipped on its head the last couple of days.

As we walked toward Billie's brothers I felt uncomfortable under Callum's scrutiny. Would he think I was just trying to ass kiss if I asked more questions about their family business? Truth was, I did want to know more about everything.

Braden waved to the trucks pulling away from the field, as Callum's gaze seemed to burn into mine.

"You want a turn, Billie?" Braden said around a smile, and I got the impression that he was the more lenient brother.

"Yeah," Billie said in an excited voice. "Dean does too."

"Is that right?" Callum said and I felt a blush creep across my cheeks.

11

DEAN

"Well," I said, attempting to keep my gaze averted from Callum's eyes because damn did this man lure me right in. "Billie kind of twisted my arm."

Callum's lip curved in a smirk as he watched Billie and Braden head up to the first level tier. Billie wasted no time getting right to the task, maybe because he knew Callum was distracted.

"Can I use the Rugar Red Label?" Billie asked with a sense of awe in his voice.

I drew closer to the steps to watch Billie more closely. If I was going to do this, I needed to figure out what the hell I was getting myself into.

"You guys built this structure?" I asked Callum once I reached the top of the very sturdy staircase.

"I helped my daddy when I was a teen," he said coming up behind me. "We weatherproof it every year to make sure it lasts."

I looked closely at the design of the different level decks. "Impressive."

"How's that?" he asked as his arm brushed against my shoulder.

"A lot of things around here look hand built and well preserved,"

I said, getting a good view of the property from up here, which was a different angle from Pines Ledge on our run this morning.

"In order to run a successful business, you can't have stuff falling apart," he said, like it was the simplest philosophy in the world. As we watched Billie place the earmuffs on his ears and protective goggles over his eyes, Braden handed a couple more sets to Callum. "You might want to wear these."

Billie began shooting at the target and from where I was standing seemed to have decent aim. He was smiling ear-to-ear and high-fiving Braden after every round of three shots as he moved through the deck levels away from us.

"Billie showed me the sugar cane field," I said, as I adjusted the gear on my ears to help blot out the sound.

Callum's eyebrows rose but he didn't say anything, probably wondering why the hell I was curious about the dead zone in the first place.

"You've got to keep up with weeding and maybe try chicken manure next time," I said, feeling self-conscious all of a sudden. I waited for the fallout from Callum, who was sure to have some sort of flippant remark.

I knew by now he would think I was trying to outwit or lecture him, but I was only in pursuit of an intelligent conversation. At least that was what I told myself. Yeah, he pushed my buttons, but on some level I must've enjoyed our discussions as well as our contact or I wouldn't continually try to seek him out.

"Is that what you learn in them fancy biology labs?" he asked, as he placed the shielding glasses over his eyes.

"Amongst other things," I said, refusing to be uncomfortable or to back down. "I also want to go back to the field and take a closer look. I think you might have a problem with *Schistocerca americana*, otherwise known as the American grasshopper."

"Say what?" Callum said, his mouth dropping open.

"Believe it or not they can cause damage to sugar cane crops.

It looked like they had chewed the leaves down to the root," I said. "That probably helped the plant lose most of its photosynthetic tissue and die."

"Holy Christ," Callum said with something like awe in his eyes. I'd admit, I liked seeing it there. "I have a degree in agriculture and even I didn't know that."

"You have a degree?" I asked, and as soon as I said the words I knew it had come out all wrong. Mouth, insert foot. "What I mean is—"

"Let me guess," he said, gritting his teeth. "You assumed I was an uneducated redneck?"

"No, Callum," I said, shaking my head fervently. "I don't think that of you at all. You...well...you're probably one of the smartest people I've ever met."

I held in my gasp wondering why in the hell I had blurted that out. A line of crimson spread across his neck as we stared each other down, both of us breathing heavily from the exchange.

"Come on then," he said, his voice tempering. "I'll show you how to shoot using the twenty-eight gauge."

He reached for the shotgun that had been leaning against the railing and demonstrated a hold for me. Then he stood behind me, as he positioned the rifle on my shoulder.

"You just aim and shoot," he said, and I felt his breath against my hairline. "Though you might be better off at the target range for your first time out, because the gear is more stable and built for beginner's practice."

He leaned over to help me adjust my fingers on the trigger. I could smell him. Pine and earth and musk. He wore his black baseball cap today and the brim slid across my ear.

A shiver raced through me as his hand rested heavily on my shoulder. It was large and warm and it made me want to know what it would feel like to be wrapped up in his embrace.

He motioned to Braden on the ground below and he pushed some button to begin the practice round.

"Pull the lever as soon as you see the object," he said, his voice thick. "And watch for the recoil."

He stepped back and as the clay shot up in the air, I jerked the trigger, and nearly flew back against his chest. "Holy shit, that's powerful."

I totally missed the target, but firing that weapon was heady regardless. I could actually understand why it might prove addicting. I mean, if I can shoot at enemy targets in Call of Duty on the Xbox, in person was way more exhilarating.

Except that animals were not the enemy, unless they were a threat of some sort. Neither were humans. But these clay targets could be.

"On your next pull," Callum said, positioning my fingers again. His front was against my back and hell if I didn't plump up a bit behind my zipper. "Hold it more firmly right here. Or your shoulder is going to be killing you."

And holy fuck, there it was. No way could I mistake it. Callum had a boner.

It felt like his heartbeat was playing chase with my own as the blood rushed my eardrums. I wanted him to take me right there. For his lips to press into my neck, his fingertips to leave indentations on my skin.

A hum burst from my throat before I could even stop myself.

"Shit," I heard him swear under his breath as he pulled back.

I had no idea how to even respond to my seductive noise or his thickening length, so I chose to ignore it. Maybe it was....hell I didn't know. Maybe shooting got him excited. I was feeling pretty high myself in that moment.

I shot a couple more rounds as Callum stood further back, allowing me plenty of room. With him a distance away, I felt like I could breathe again. I didn't dare look at him. Who knew what in the fuck was going on in his head?

I missed the second round of targets, but on the next try, I got a corner of one of them.

"There you go," Callum said but kept his eyes averted from me.

As I caught my breath and stretched out my shoulder, I heard the sound of a truck pulling up. It was the same kind as last night, but this time a younger man jumped out.

"Who's that?" I asked over my shoulder.

"That's the infamous Jerry," Callum said in a gruff voice.

"I can see the appeal," I said, admiring his lean physique and handsome face. What was it with country boys? I could feel Callum staring at me for that remark. Damn. "I mean..."

"Callum, what's up?" Jerry shouted from down below. He watched as Billie shot again. "Nice one, Billie."

Callum nodded, looking down at his neighbor. "Jerry."

"Just stopped by to see if you need help with the wedding prep," he said and then made eye contact with me. "Who have we got here?"

Well this should be interesting. I looked at Callum who seemed to be formulating his response.

"Jerry, meet Dean," he said in a tight voice. "Dean is here as Cassie's guest. He's her date for the wedding."

Jerry assessed me, his lips drawn in a tight line, before finally throwing me a halfhearted wave. "Nice to meet you."

"You as well," I said as he made his way to the other side of the wobble deck to speak to Braden and Billie.

"Dude's got it bad, huh?" I asked Callum as we watched him from the far end.

"I see it as a rejection thing," Callum said, removing his protective gear and I followed suit. "Cassie broke up with him and the guy can't get over himself. Doesn't make much sense since he's got plenty lined up to take her place."

"Maybe he knows she's special," I said, and something shuttered in Callum's gaze as he watched me. "Just because you've got lots of options or even opportunities doesn't mean they all feel right."

"For sure," Callum said out of the corner of his mouth, thinking something through. I was desperate to know exactly what it was in that moment.

"Still," I said, motioning to the other end of the deck. "Dude's got to move on."

"Just ignore him," Callum said, as he packed up our supplies and made his way down the stairs toward a small wooden shed. Guess my target practice was over.

12

CALLUM

I could not believe I got an erection at the gun range. Damn, the way Dean smelled. All masculine with a hint of his shampoo, some kind of grapefruit I would've guessed.

He didn't even attempt to pull away from me. It might've been my imagination or he was simply embarrassed for me.

But his harsh breaths and the sound he made in the very back of his throat. Maybe he was...fuck, I don't even know. My emotions were all over the map.

Why was I drawn to this man? I'd seen plenty of hot guys over the years, but I didn't get a boner over all of them. Maybe it was because he seemed so deeply opposed to our way of life and I wanted to prove him wrong at every turn.

After some necessary trimming of hedges, the rest of the day was spent around the cabin, cleaning up after the last group and prepping for our relatives. Cassie had brought Dean over to see the rooms and she pointed out the sawmill near the vegetable garden when he asked who had made some of the storage sheds on the property.

"Callum constructed all of these chairs and tables, too,"

Cassie said with a lilt of pride in her voice and I felt a funny twinge in my chest.

"Seriously?" Dean asked with awe in his voice. "They're amazing."

"Yep," she said. "He loves working in the woodshop and even sells some of the pieces in town at Aunt June's furniture store."

Aunt June was my mother's sister, so she might've just been doing me a favor, but according to her my pieces sold like hotcakes, and she was always harping on me to make more. If only I could find some extra time without having to burn the midnight oil.

I felt Dean's eyes on me but I kept my gaze fixed on the hardwood floor as I swept along the baseboards. Guess he didn't see me as some big dumb hunter after all. He said as much to me this morning. And damn if that didn't make my brain short-circuit.

"There's a smokehouse too?" I heard Dean ask after I stepped outside to sweep the porch. He was standing at the screen door looking outside as I moved the rocking chairs out of my path.

"Right," Cassie said. "Grammy smokes fish that we catch from the lake. But we can smoke meat as well."

"What kind of meat?" he asked, and I could just picture him holding back a cringe. "The quail and deer from your property?"

"For your information," Cassie said in a singsong voice, as if they had these kinds of debates all the time. And maybe they did, though I still suspected something was off about their relationship. Or maybe I just wanted to see it that way. "Deer overpopulate and cause accidents out on the road. Instead of the county sending out their sharpshooters to control the excess, true hunters will use that meat to feed their families."

"Aren't there more humane ways?" he asked. "Like...the other day I read about a medical procedure vets can do on the females so they can't reproduce."

"It's called sterilization," Cassie said, rolling her eyes at her scientist boyfriend. "There would still be human intervention in that method. Plus cost involved."

"True," Dean said, sighing in resignation. "What did the deer do before humans came along to help them handle their own population?"

I couldn't even stop myself. Every time I heard his voice, some imaginary button was triggered deep inside, making me want to interact with him. Shake him. Yell at him. Kiss the shit out of him. Fuck. I really shouldn't have been this attracted to some guy my sister brought as her date.

"They would get taken out by larger species. Life cycle. Survival of the fittest. That was before there were highways, train tracks, houses, and businesses," I said, trying to steady my voice. "You can't have it both ways. Either you're in favor of progress or you want to go back to living in the cave man days. Give up your fancy smart phone and fend for yourself."

"Well said," Dean mumbled. Instead of getting angry and coming back with an offhanded remark his features tempered. "Still doesn't explain why humans need to eat the meat of an animal or use their coat to create things. It's barbaric."

"Says the man who probably owns a pair or two of leather shoes. So you want us all to run around eating nuts and berries and tofu. You'd have the farmers give up their livelihood—the cattle and sheep trade," I said in exasperation. "Farmers are probably our most important resource in this country, and plenty of people forget that."

"There are other ways—"

"What kind of vegetarian are you anyway—" I said, shoving my hand in my pocket before I throttled him. "You still eat dairy?"

His face had turned tomato red like he was going to explode at a moment's notice. "I try not to, not if I can help it, but—"

"Callum!" Cassie started in on me, but I held up my hand.

"I'm done," I grumbled, replacing the broom and heading to

my truck. "Guess you won't be trying Billie's homemade ice cream tonight."

I buried myself in the office with paperwork until suppertime while I listened to a ball game on the radio. Or maybe I was just hiding. What was it about Dean that got under my skin? I understood vegetarians in principle. I actually couldn't consume any gamey meat myself. I didn't have the palate for it.

But I didn't want Dean to have the impression that we were savages or something.

By the time dinner rolled around I realized I hadn't eaten since breakfast.

When I entered the kitchen, Dean and Billie had their heads bent over some game on the iPad. Dean was wearing his sexy black frames, probably so he could see the smaller screen.

I wanted to grab him by the shirt and kiss him senseless. Then give him head while he wore only those eyeglasses.

The two of them were chuckling over something on the monitor and I felt a pang in my gut. My brother was seen as different and fragile to the outside world. But Dean had marched right in and warmed to him instantly.

"Anything I can help with, Grammy?" I asked, avoiding eye contact with Dean. I'd admit I was embarrassed about how often I spouted off at him. I'd blame it on sexual frustration if I knew that was the only reason.

"Dean and Billie helped set the table," Grammy said. "But how about you get everybody's drink orders? Right after you ring the dinner bell."

"I want to do it!" Billie jumped up and rushed past me out to the porch.

Grammy and I watched him from the screen door and I felt Dean move in beside me.

"How long has that bell been in your family?" he asked.

"At least a hundred years," Grammy said, smiling as Billie

yanked on the substantial gold chain. "My mother used to come from the fields by the sound of those chimes."

"That is amazing." Dean turned to look at her and I felt his soft breath against the side of my face. "What was in the fields?"

"Sugar cane and citrus crops were my family's highest producers at that time," she said, with a hint of pride in her voice. "They were also in the cattle trade. Even had some off-shore export deal with a farm in Cuba."

"I saw some orange trees out there," Dean said. "Why did your family abandon the cattle trade?"

"Not sure I know the real answer," she said, watching Billie as he waved to Cassie. "The next generation decided to go in a different direction. I suppose they weren't true farmers, so they moved on to other things."

As my family began filing in for dinner, I took drink orders. My father always saved hard liquor for after dinner, so I knew he'd ask for some milk. But Billie and Braden always requested soda. I expected for Dean to ask for water, same as Cassie, who had come in from fertilizing some of the newer perennials we had planted in the front garden.

So when Dean requested diet soda, my eyebrows knit together. He held his tongue as if ready for a new debate. But I couldn't pick a fight with the sexy man about everything—even about choosing to put synthetic chemicals into his body—just because I wanted him in my bed so badly.

Not only could you not change somebody's views or misconceptions overnight, you absolutely were hopeless at attempting to change anybody's sexuality. If only the naysayers in this conservative town realized that.

"What does your family do, Dean?" Grammy asked, once we were all situated around the table.

"My father is an advertising executive in New Jersey," he mumbled, his cheeks coloring. Why did that embarrass him? Was it because it sounded so pretentious?

"Why didn't you join the business?" This question came from my father.

Cassie was trying to throw Daddy some big eyes, but he ignored her while he devoured his pork tenderloin dinner. Braden's eyes were slightly glazed over, never really giving Cassie's friends any real attention, unless they were going to stick around for a while. Either that or his mind was on his list of chores, which was plentiful.

"I just..." Dean said, bracing his fork until his knuckles turned white. "Sometimes you can have completely different interests than your parents do."

Dad grunted at that over his glass of milk and I noticed how Cassie reached for Dean's hand beneath the table. Must've been a sore subject for him. When Dean adjusted his legs, I felt his foot skim absently over mine, seeking room, and I nearly jumped out of my skin. Man, I needed to get a grip.

"And different relationships as well," Dean continued as he glanced around the table, making eye contact with everybody but me. "You guys are lucky. It feels so comfortable and authentic here."

"Even if I'm serving meat at this table?" Grammy asked, chuckling. "Don't worry, I made an extra vegetable for you. Those green beans are straight from our garden."

"I appreciate that," Dean said, biting his lip, and suddenly I felt terrible for my earlier comments. What in the fuck was wrong with me? That wasn't how you treated a guest in the house. My mother would've been ashamed of me.

"I have homemade ice cream for dessert," Billie said excitedly. "French vanilla."

He loved trying new recipes with the secondhand ice cream machine he bought a couple of years ago off a dairy farmer.

"Maybe you should have Dean try your homemade granita instead?" I offered the slushy dessert as an alternative, knowing it was only made with simple syrup. Both Grammy and Cassie's eyebrows shot up, understanding dawning that I was attempting to arrange a truce.

Dean stared at me, gratitude and something else I couldn't identify in his eyes. "Actually, if Billie made that ice cream, I'd love to taste it."

Dean and I shared a private smile across the table, both raising our imaginary white flags.

13

DEAN

I had stayed up late last night playing Xbox with Billie who babbled on about everything under the sun. He let it slip that Callum was the gentlest brother, and that he rarely left the preserve for long, and that information had thrown me for a loop.

He also spouted off about how Braden's girlfriend wasn't so friendly to him, how his dad worked too hard, and how Cassie promised he could visit her in the city.

If I wanted to know all about the Montgomery family, Billie was my go-to guy.

At one point, Callum stumbled out of bed to pour himself a glass of water from the kitchen sink.

"You guys are still up?" he asked in a groggy voice while rubbing the sleep out of his bleary eyes.

I ignored the fact that he only wore a pair of navy boxer shorts. Holy shit, that body of his. "Do you realize that your brother produced a replica of Yankee Stadium?"

"I do," he said, yawning. "I helped create part of it."

I inhaled a breath. I didn't know what I was thinking; maybe that Callum wouldn't have the patience to sit with Billie for hours on end.

"Callum loves baseball, even played it in high school," Billie said. "He always has a game on the radio."

I stared at Callum, imagining him in tight polyester pants. "Do you have a favorite team?"

Before he could get his answer out, Billie jumped in. "Obviously it's New York."

I should've guessed from the vintage looking ball cap he sometimes wore. The team colors were blue, gray, and white, so the black had thrown me off. I suppose they were made in plenty of shades as long as they sold.

"But we never finished building the ballpark," Billie said. "So Dean agreed to help."

Callum studied the screen. "Looks good."

I tried not to stare at his bare skin. At the line of freckles across his collarbone and the smattering of hair down the center of his chest. How his shoulders were wide but his waist was narrow. I longed to trace my tongue along every delicious inch.

As if he could read my thoughts, his nipples tightened into stiff knots. He turned suddenly, rubbing at the back of his neck, as if realizing for the very first time how he was dressed in front of a houseguest.

"Not much longer, Billie," he said over his shoulder as he practically fled the room. "We've got a big day tomorrow."

"We're about done here," I said, shifting to adjust myself. "Didn't mean to keep him up."

"Please," Billie whispered conspiratorially. "Callum is all about following the rules. We're fine."

Billie spoke of Callum as if he was a parent figure. It made me snicker. This family's dynamics were certainly interesting.

* * *

MY ALARM WOKE me out of a deep sleep. For a second I didn't remember where in the hell I was.

I finally rolled out of bed, numbly slipped on my clothes, and headed for a quick bathroom trip where I brushed my teeth and splashed water on my face.

I padded toward the kitchen and quietly slipped out the door.

"You're late," Callum said, stretching on the grass. Seeing him waiting there both thrilled and infuriated me at the same time.

"I told you I don't need a babysitter," I muttered.

"Never said you did," he said with a hint of haughtiness in his tone. "Besides, I could use another run."

I watched as Callum gritted his teeth working his hamstrings. He was sore, which either meant he pushed himself too far, or wasn't a regular runner. I didn't know what to make of that.

My heart thrashed in my chest as I considered him. I was completely attracted to Callum but I wanted to throttle him at the same time. I was nearly desperate to know what his story was, especially since he got a hard-on at the shooting range when pressed up against me. But I also needed to keep my distance because I was supposed to be here as Cassie's guest.

"Suit yourself," I grunted while extending my calf muscles.

I skipped the other warm-up exercises and headed for the trail, not giving Callum a second glance. I wasn't sure what his motive was but I was ready to hit the ground running, if anything, to burn off this pent up sexual frustration.

In another minute Callum caught up to me and we ran side-by-side for a while. I figured he'd razz me for taking off without him, but he merely stared straight ahead, getting his breathing under control.

A yawn burst from my lips and I attempted to cover it up with the back of my hand.

"You guys stay up much longer?" he mumbled.

"About thirty minutes more," I said, recalling how it was me who had called it a day. I suspected Billie could've stayed up all night, and then slept all morning. But I imagined Callum grumbling if he knew his brother hadn't gone to bed, so I sent us both packing. Why his opinion mattered to me, I didn't quite have a handle on yet.

"You're really good with him," Callum said in his side view.

"He's easy to like," I said, quirking my shoulder. "I was close with my brother, Shawn, before he died from Leukemia."

Callum's feet faltered. "Fuck, I'm sorry."

"No, it's okay. I've had years to come to terms with it," I said. "My family handled it all weird, though. My dad threw himself even harder into work and my mom volunteered for all of these charities to keep herself occupied."

"What did you do?" he asked, studying me as the trail veered east.

Nobody had ever asked me that question before and I had to consider my answer carefully.

"I got brave, I guess," I said, wondering if he would think my response sounded lame. "Told myself I was going to be me, no matter what."

His breaths became more ragged as he looked toward the shrubs. I didn't know if my reply had triggered something for him, but I continued with my revelation anyway because it was enlightening for me as well.

"I did what made me feel good. Like going back for my master's," I said. "Not what my dad wanted."

His eyebrows shot to his hairline. "Your father doesn't believe in your research?"

"In theory, sure. Maybe if I was doing cancer exploration." I sighed. "But most university labs depend on grants. You can be shut down at any time. The pay is good, but not great. Not up to his standards, at least."

"Why study entomology?" he asked. My stride wavered

because his extensive knowledge of random subjects always took me by surprise. If I didn't know any better, Callum was a closet bookworm. Or at least an avid World Wide Web surfer.

"I don't know," I said. "I actually thought I'd go into the medical track. Immunology or infectious disease. You know, helping find cures for insect to human contact."

"Like the West Nile virus or Rocky Mountain spotted fever?" he asked with a smirk. Smarty pants, showing me up.

"Right," I said. "But then I kind of fell into agricultural and biochemistry research with one of my favorite professors. I've gone on a couple of short woodland trips with him already. Truth is, I've always wanted to live somewhere away from the city. As long as there was a metropolis near by."

"You can take the city boy out of the country, but not—"

"Exactly," I said laughing. "I mean, honestly, I would work in any lab that offered something of interest. But in the long run, I'd love to be in a wide-open space, at least for part of the year. Some of my favorite vacations involved camping and hiking in the mountains."

"Can't beat the mountains," Callum said.

"Did you always know you'd stay right here?" I asked him. "In this town?"

A flash of discomfort crossed his features. "Mostly, yeah. It's not without its challenges. I enjoy my family, working with them, and Billie..."

He trailed off as if unable to say the words.

"He needs you," I said simply.

I heard a rough intake of breath as his eyes shot to mine and the vulnerability in his gaze said it all. He couldn't leave Billie. *Wouldn't.* Even though he had plenty of family around. Somehow he felt responsible for raising him. And in that moment, Callum was more stunning than ever before.

"Billie speaks very highly of you, you know," I said. "He also claims you never get out."

I cringed, hoping again that I hadn't said the wrong thing. What he did in his spare time was none of my damn business.

The same look of anguish lined his brow and I felt terrible for saying anything at all. Then it was gone and he pounded the trail harder.

He burst ahead of me up the incline to Pines Ledge, as if he needed to work whatever had upset him out of his system.

I leaned against the large evergreen near the rock to catch my breath and fished my water bottle from my pack to guzzle. I lifted my shirt to wipe my face because I was burning up and then pulled it off my shoulders to tuck inside my shorts.

When I glanced over at Callum, he paced along the edge of the railing, watching me with a troubled look. The tension in the air grew thick and I wanted to reach out to him, to touch and soothe him.

He turned away and stripped his own shirt over his neck. His strong shoulders and back muscles flexed as if he were merely holding everything inside. All the molecules between us seemed to swirl and ignite, choking off my airway.

A noise I couldn't contain escaped my throat. Something that sounded like *nhh*. I squeezed my lids shut and heard him shift.

When I opened my eyes, he was facing my way and had taken a step closer. We were both breathing hard from our run and maybe some other things as well. Things I didn't quite grasp. I refused to look down at his shorts to see if he was at half-mast like me.

It seemed like an eternity passed between us as our gazes stayed fastened together. My brain was short-circuiting wondering if I was only imagining the longing in his eyes. Or if maybe it was simply a reflection of my own.

Callum stalked toward me, forcing my shoulders against the tree, and slammed his mouth over mine. I groaned into the bruising kiss and my hands flew up to grip his hair.

He tasted like Callum—pine and salt and earth and it was so

heady, I was having trouble processing all the amazing sensations at once. I just knew I wanted more.

His tongue lapped greedily against mine and my fingers curled as I mashed my lips harder against his.

I thrust my tongue deep inside his mouth fully tasting all of him.

He moaned, sinking his body against mine. The bark of the pine dug into my back and I could feel his enormous cock against my stomach.

He swiped his tongue across my bottom lip and then bit down, sucking with abandon. I whimpered and shifted my hip trying to align our stiff cocks, to feel even more of him.

He dragged his mouth away and blinked, as if snapping out of the crazy spell we were under. I was in a daze, unable to compute having been kissed by him, but absolutely wanting it to happen again.

"Oh shit," he grunted out. "I...you...damn, my sister. What did I do?"

He backed away from me, anguish blazing in his eyes.

I raised a shaky hand to my neck. "No, wait, you don't have to—"

He took off running down the path.

I stood there stunned a moment before bolting after him in a half jog. No way I'd catch up with him now. But I'd find him as soon as I got there. He needed to know I was gay because obviously he was too, or he was only now realizing it.

Damn, had that been his first time kissing a man? Sure hadn't felt that way.

As my feet pounded the trail, a lot of things were clicking into place like the pieces of an elaborate puzzle. How he rarely left the preserve, never had a girlfriend, and seemed to have a thunderstorm of conflicting emotions swirling inside him.

I picked up my pace, hoping the house was still quiet when I returned. I'd find him and talk it through. I wanted more of that kiss. More of everything.

14

CALLUM

Fucking hell. What was I thinking? I just kissed my sister's boyfriend. So not cool.

I jogged all the way home and then jumped in my pickup and drove the heck out of there. The light was on in the kitchen so I knew Grammy or Daddy were just waking up and I didn't want to face anybody right now. I needed time to process things.

Was Dean bisexual? Hadn't he kissed me back? I shuddered remembering how he groaned against me. How his tongue felt in my mouth. I pushed down at my cock with the heel of my hand.

As soon as I got on the main road, I turned up the radio and just kept driving, thinking about everything and nothing all at once. How I wish I could've met Dean under different circumstances. Because he appeared to see right inside me. To drag things out of me.

Though he would've nonetheless been some uptight city boy that rubbed me the wrong way. But hell, I'd still want to fuck him. Or have him fuck me. I wasn't picky. Or I sure wouldn't be when it came to him.

And then what? It wasn't like we could hook up again after

that. But maybe having him one time would've been enough. He lived in a different state. And besides, I couldn't be with anybody, not if I continued running the business. It always came back to that. The reason I had to hide. I couldn't forgive myself if I messed with my family's livelihood.

Maybe this was more about sexual frustration. If I took care of business, I might feel a whole hell of a lot better. But as it was now, my skin was buzzing from having Dean's hands and mouth on me.

I fished out my phone and considered calling Jason for a hookup. He'd just be waking up for work. I could ask him to get together this weekend. But maybe he'd make an exception and meet me sooner. Like today.

But then I'd be thinking about somebody else and that wouldn't be fair. Still, he had become a good friend, so I phoned him anyway.

"Well this is an early surprise," Jason answered in a groggy voice.

"Yeah," I said grimacing, regretting my decision immediately. How desperate did I sound? "Sorry, I'm on the road picking up some extra chairs for the wedding reception and figured you'd be up."

At least that was true enough. While I was out, I'd get an errand or two out of the way. We had plenty of wooden chairs that we used for our hunting guests, but there weren't enough to cover this occasion, which called for about a hundred and twenty guests.

I heard a male voice in the background. Shit, Jason had company.

"Oh damn," I said. "My bad. You're not alone."

"It's okay." I heard some movement, some ruffling of sheets maybe, and I pictured Jason climbing out of bed. Fuck, this was awkward. "Sounds like you might need a sympathetic ear."

"No worries, I'm going to let you go—"

"Stop it," he said, exasperated. "You're my friend and you called for a reason. Let's talk."

My shoulders relaxed against the seat. "I forget how well you can read me sometimes."

Jason laughed and it was a rich throaty sound. "Years of practice."

He and I had been friends since our first year in college, where we came out to each other. He pretty much taught me how to be a lover. The difference between us, however, was that he was living out in the open as a gay man and I was not.

"What's on your mind, Callum?" he asked. "I can tell something's bugging you."

I turned down a side street toward the party center warehouse that had our supplies on reserve. "We have guests out at the preserve. Cassie brought a date."

"Ah, I see where this is leading," he said with a smile in his voice. "Got the hots for the guy?"

Since the warehouse didn't open for another twenty minutes, I hitched a right at the entrance and pulled into a far space in the empty lot to concentrate on this conversation.

"I did something stupid." I winced and rubbed my hand over my face. If it was so mortifying, then why was my dick still hard? "I was feeling vibes from him the past couple of days..."

"Oh God," Jason blurted out. "You didn't screw your sister's date, did you?"

"No way." Though, would that really have been out of the question? The man had me so worked up. The thought was certainly there. Fuck. "But I...I kissed him."

"And?" he asked. I heard the sound of water running in the sink. "Did he kiss you back?"

"Yeah. God, yeah." He wanted it as much as I did. That noise that came out of his throat. A cross between a whimper and a groan. Just like at the gun range yesterday.

"So what's the problem?" Jason asked.

"Besides the fact that he's supposed to be with Cassie?" I asked incredulously. Were we even on the same page? "I freaked as soon as I realized what I had done and ran away."

"You didn't mention that he and Cassie were serious. Obviously he swings both ways," Jason said. "Don't be so hard on yourself. You are living quite a monk life out there."

I ignored his monk comment. I've heard it too many times to count and besides, there was little I could do about it. "How the hell am I going to face him?"

"Head on, like an adult," he said. "You just need to talk to him about it. Doesn't sound like you were forcing your tongue down his throat."

"You're right," I said and then there was an elongated patch of silence.

I could hear Jason sipping on something, probably his morning coffee, and I felt bad that I had kept him so long, especially if his one-night stand hadn't left yet. Maybe they had time for one more quickie and I was being a fucking cock block.

So I got straight to the point.

"I was actually wondering if maybe we could meet up sometime soon," I said, knowing I probably sounded desperate by this point. But that was how it always worked with Jason. He knew the way I operated—that I would work my ass off for weeks on the preserve and then need to get laid. If he wasn't available, then I'd chance it at one of the bars, but that didn't always work out so well.

I could hear the hesitation in his voice and I realized how very wrong this whole conversation was. I was asking him to meet me while he had somebody at his place.

But we had always been casual. So maybe his hookup wasn't. "Forget I said that."

"No, it's cool. But you screwing around with somebody else is probably not going to solve your problem," he said. "If you're hot for someone then you just are. There won't be a stand-in that will replace them no matter what you tell yourself."

"Yeah," I sighed, sliding my fingers around the steering wheel. "You're probably right."

I heard his visitor murmur in the background and Jason lightly chuckled.

"Is that how you feel about the guy you're with now?" I asked, tentatively.

"I guess so, yeah." There was a dreamy quality to his voice.

"Happy for you," I said, but my stomach churned. Not because I wanted to be the one to make Jason feel that. But because I would never have that with anybody. Except that was something I was willing to live with.

"You know what I'm going to say," Jason bit out. "Your family loves you—they'd get used to the idea. Especially Cassie."

"It could affect our business contacts," I said. "You know how backwards and conservative most folks in that town are. If they knew a queer was running Shady Pines—"

"So you're going to hide for the sake of the family business?" he asked. Same argument, different day. "You're going to grow to be a very unsatisfied man."

Already am.

"I know," I said, resigned to my station in life. "Thanks for the talk. Sorry I busted in on your time with him. What's his name by the way?"

"Brian," he said, his voice hitching a little.

"Well Brian has got himself a great guy," I said. "Catch you later."

I loaded most of the extra chairs for the wedding in the bed of my truck. But it would take a couple of trips. Then I drove across town to pick up a keg of beer.

When I finally made my way back home I wasn't any clearer about what I needed to do in this situation. Maybe if I ignored it, it would go away.

15

DEAN

Callum had been gone for a couple of hours. I took a shower, had breakfast with Billie and Grammy, and attempted to act casual in front of Cassie and her family. I couldn't out her brother to her, it wasn't my place.

"You okay?" Cassie asked out on the porch where I had gone to catch a breather. "You seem on edge."

"Fine." I needed to talk to Callum. Make sure he didn't think he corrupted me or made me do something I didn't want to do. Or worse—that I had cheated on his sister. I felt terrible not saying something to Cassie but I couldn't until I spoke to Callum first.

When Callum finally strode through the door, I was at the kitchen table with Billie, canning some strawberries that were leftover from the garden. Cassie was at the cabin with her grandmother getting the rooms ready for guests. When I asked if I could help, she said they could use my assistance later.

My hands froze on the glass container as Callum looked over at me. He was still in the clothes from our morning jog and his skin looked clammy, like he was overheated from his drive.

As he stared at me across the room, his eyes snagged on my lips before moving up to my eyes.

My mouth opened to ask if I could talk to him, but he spoke directly over me. "Billie, I picked up the chairs for the wedding. Where're Braden and Daddy?"

"Daddy's mowing and Braden is tending to the chickens." I thought I had heard a rooster the last couple of mornings. That explained it. What didn't this family do?

Callum nodded. "Going to jump in the shower and then you can help me set up in the field."

As he trudged toward the hallway, I panicked, wondering whether he would ignore me all day. We needed to talk about what happened.

"Callum," I barked out, my frustration boiling over. He stopped at the sound of my voice but didn't turn around to face me. "Um....I wanted to ask your advice on something."

His shoulders tensed. "When I have time."

He kept walking and after another minute, the shower turned on down the hall.

Billie was staring at me with an odd expression on his face and I felt my cheeks heat up.

"Callum gets like that," Billie said, spooning the last of the sweet preserve mixture into the jars.

"Like what?" I asked as I picked up the rag and wiped at a spill on the table.

"Grumpy," he said, without hesitation. "Sometimes there's stuff on his mind and he needs to work through it by going off on his own or doing lots of work. And when he's out chopping wood? You really let him be."

The visual of Callum chopping wood, shirtless and sweaty, made my eyes nearly cross. Fuck.

But what Billie said was beginning to make a ton of sense to me. We began screwing on all the lids but I could hardly concentrate because my mind was racing.

When I finally heard the water shut off, I took that as my opportunity to do something about this tension between us. I could not deal with this all day. The last two hours had about killed me.

I wanted to hurry before I lost my chance but I didn't want to appear overeager to Billie.

"Going to go see who needs help," I said, standing up. "Grabbing my sneakers."

I refrained from sprinting to my room and stood awkwardly on the threshold as if I was stalking him. But with Billie being the only Montgomery member in the house, this was my only shot.

When Callum didn't emerge after another minute, I stepped forward and gave his door one quick rap with my knuckles.

When he swung it open, surprise didn't register on his face, only anxiety as he bent his head and looked down the hall to make certain we were alone.

He had changed into a blue Yankees T-shirt, his hair was wet, and his eyes were a dull shade of amber. They appeared to change according to his mood. Light and brilliant when he was smiling, dark and murky when he was sullen.

"Please," I mouthed, my knees practically giving out.

He nodded and stepped aside, closing the door behind me.

His room was modern and clean, as if it were a separate wing in this traditional farmhouse. His bedding was a dark taupe color, his walls were teal blue and at a quick glance he had some framed vintage photos of major league baseball parks hanging on a couple of the walls.

On a dresser in the corner of the room, there was a beat up baseball housed in a delicate glass box, which may have held great meaning. It was resting alongside his black ball cap that he seemed to be so fond of.

When he saw what my eyes had snagged on he said, "My grandfather was in the minor leagues and that was his hundredth home run ball. Grammy gave it to me."

I nodded and then opened my mouth to speak. "Callum—"

"Look, I'm sorry," he blurted out before I could finish my thought. "I should have never done that. It was out of line. You're here with my sister and damn, she...you..."

He squeezed his eyes shut and rushed his fingers through his hair.

"Stop," I said in a gentle voice, attempting to calm him down and alleviate his guilt. "Let me talk for a second."

He eyed me warily, but then conceded. "Okay."

I stepped closer to him because I couldn't resist. He smelled so good. Clean and soapy and earthy. Callum didn't pull back—simply stayed put watching me.

"I wanted you to do that," I said, staring at his plump lips. "I kissed you back, remember?"

"Then why the hell are you with my sister?" His eyes narrowed into slits and I thought for a second that he might slug me. "I don't want her to be hurt because of something we did."

"I don't either." I held up my hands in a surrender position and watched his fists closely. "But you've got to understand. Cassie won't be upset."

He took a step back, outrage in his face. "How could you—"

"I'm gay," I said, finally getting the words out. The relief was like a punch to the gut, and I nearly sagged against him.

"What?" Callum looked struck dumb, which confused me. Why else would I kiss him? Unless he thought I was bi or bi curious. "Does my sister..."

"Yes, she knows," I said, taking a step closer to him. "We're not together. I'm her friend. Her roommate actually."

His face had flushed red and it was like a slideshow of images were arranging themselves in his brain.

"I don't know what's become of your relationship with your sister," I said in a show of honesty, even though I was probably walking a thin line. "But she wanted to bring somebody with her to get Jerry off her trail, and she didn't think she could share that with anybody."

He bit his lip and looked down at his feet, mumbling, "You don't know anything. Who are you to question...?"

"I don't want to argue with you again," I said. "My point is that, if you were honest with Cassie, she would understand. I told her the same thing about you."

"Cassie and me," he stuttered out. "It's been years...I feel like I don't know her anymore."

"Living in the city is not the same as down here. We have plenty of gay friends," I said. "Still, she's the same sister you loved growing up. She's smart and open and accepting. I can tell she misses you."

His face paled at my words and he looked just as regretful.

"Look, I feel terrible keeping this from Cassie, she's my best friend. But it's not my place to out you," I said. "You've been hiding for a long time."

Stepping forward, I curled my fingers around his neck, drawing our foreheads together. I could feel him trembling and I ached to comfort him.

"I wanted to kiss you the moment I laid eyes on you," I whispered.

"Thought you were just some arrogant city boy rolling your eyes at us country folk," he said. "You frustrated me right quick. But then all I thought about were your lips. How they would taste."

"And how do they taste?" I asked, my mouth nearly brushing against his.

"Incredible," he murmured, and when his lips caressed mine in a barely there kiss, they tingled. I was solid as marble now, his sexy words cranking me up so damn high.

I swiped my tongue against his bottom lip and he groaned. "Is this okay?"

I pulled his lip into my mouth and sucked, releasing it to look up at him. "Because if it's too much or you don't want—"

"God, no. Please." We tapped lips once, twice, my tongue darted out to glide lightly against his and then we were full on kissing.

I was making out with Cassie's brother. Right in her family's home. Holy fuck.

His hands were skimming up and down my neck and shoulders and then grabbing at my hair. I felt engulfed by the sheer enormity of his size. Hot damn, he was making me horny as hell.

"Fuck, you're driving me wild," he said, dragging his mouth away from mine. "I want you so bad."

"Likewise," I said, my fingers gripping the back of his shirt, yanking him flush against me.

And then we were devouring each other again as he backed me to the closet door, thrusting his groin against mine. "I swear I could come just like this."

He seized my fingers and hauled them above my head as I groaned, the back of my head knocking the wood, delirious from his lips and smell and body pinning me down.

The sound of a cabinet banging and voices griping echoed from the kitchen.

He dragged his mouth away and looked behind him to the door. "Shit."

"Does anybody know?" I asked, straightening myself, missing his warmth immediately. I liked seeing his swollen lips and his mussed up hair. His eyes transforming to a brilliant caramel shade. I liked that I had done that to him.

"Only one friend in town named Jason," he said, his eyes wide and round, fear settling back in between us.

I stepped away from the door. "Somebody you're with?"

"Of course not," he snapped. "I would never be doing this if I...we've hooked up before, that's it."

"Understood," I said. "Sorry, you don't need to explain anything to me. I won't be here for much longer anyway. After this week, I'm gone."

Something shuttered in his gaze as we stared each other down. "Then I guess we need to make the most of it."

16

CALLUM

Holy fuck, what the hell was happening here?

I couldn't stop kissing this person who came into my room and basically blew my mind.

Dean was gay, he wanted me, and he wasn't with my sister. Cassie who, God love her, had been such a good sibling until I pulled away from her, from everybody.

I clasped my hand around Dean's neck and drew him to me again. His eyes and mouth and hands were as hungry for me as mine were for him. And I wanted to get my fill until he had to go home, which was in no time at all. I thrust aside the melancholy that sat heavy from the idea of Dean and Cassie leaving. I definitely needed to fix some things with my sister first.

I rubbed my lips against Dean's again and again until he groaned and pulled my body so tight against his there was scarcely any room between us. His tongue thrust inside my mouth and drew deep, luring me into a drugging rhythm.

I just wanted more time to keep kissing him. Because damn, the way his lips moved over mine, was pure bliss. As if there was some electric current buzzing between us and I couldn't seem to drag myself away.

The voices in the kitchen grew louder.

"Callum," Braden's voice sounded from the end of the hall. "We're about to set up the chairs and tables. Some family has already arrived."

I hauled my mouth away. Fuck, what the hell were we doing hiding in my room consuming each other? Anybody could've walked in. I took a step back, completely in a daze. Dean's eyes were glossy and he swiped his hand across his mouth.

"Be right there," I shouted to Braden and then my eyes met Dean's as we stood there panting heavily.

"What do we do?" he asked in a low register, his eyes darting to the door. I could tell the realization was setting in for him as well. It wasn't like we could simply emerge from this room hand in hand. Nobody could know what we were up to. That we were so attracted to each other, we could barely see straight. Or at least that was how I felt.

"Don't have many choices except what we're already doing," I said, the resignation settling in my voice. If we were in a different situation, in Cassie and Dean's more progressive city, this might've played out another way. Maybe Dean and I would openly hook up or even date.

The idea of that made me shiver. To actually be able to date somebody out in the open.

"You mean we go on pretending?" Dean asked, his face crumpling a bit.

"Got to," I said. "My entire family will be here. You're supposed to be with Cassie."

"Shit, you're right," he said, shaking his head and settling into the idea again. "You'll think about telling Cassie, though? She... she'd understand."

"I will," I said, heading toward the door. We needed to leave this room before somebody discovered us together. "I promise."

We spent the rest of the afternoon setting up for the ceremony and greeting my cousins Monica and Rich, along with their siblings and parents, who seemed thrilled about getting hitched tomorrow. We arranged the chairs in rows and the wedding planner showed up to organize a tent and decorations, which included an arbor and hundreds of flowers. By the time they were halfway done, the field looked magical.

For the first time ever, I considered the fact that I would never have something like this, even with the legal ruling of gay marriage. I'd never have the opportunity to be this open, to be surrounded by family and friends if I found a person I wanted to spend my life with.

When my gaze drifted to Braden, I could tell the setting was having the opposite effect, like he was dreading his girlfriend getting any bright ideas when she arrived later today.

Every time I glanced at Dean and saw his kiss-swollen lips my cock would plump back up. By this time, I was liable to go cross-eyed from the sexual tension alone.

Billie seemed to stick close to Dean's side, like he was drawn to his natural charm or friendship. It made something compress in my gut. If anyone, it was Billie who would be disappointed when Dean left. He had already grown attached to him.

"You doing okay, brother?" Cassie asked after I helped roll out the white walkway between the chairs in the aisle for the bride.

"Yeah, sure," I said. "Why?"

She looked at me as if she could see straight through me.

Remember when we used to be so close? Why did I shut her out, *everybody* out?

"I just...God, Callum," she said. "I'm only going to be here for a few more days, and I was hoping we could..."

"What?" I asked, noticing how stiff her body language had become.

"Spend some time together," she said, and then bit her lip as if she was expecting me to blow her off. My chest constricted so tight. Fuck, I had done this to her.

I placed my hand on her shoulder and felt her relax into my touch. "I'd really like that."

"Good." She blew out a breath and then turned to watch Billie helping our daddy lock away some tools in the shed. Dean was close by talking to Grammy, who stood with a tray, offering our guests some sweet tea.

"So, how do you feel about Dean?" Cassie asked and I nearly swallowed my tongue.

"Why do you ask?" I said around the boulder in my throat. Did she know? Had my gaze been seeking him out too frequently?

"Because he came here as my date?" she said, her voice dripping with sarcasm.

My pulse immediately turned it down a notch. "Yeah, sure, seems he's a good guy after all."

She cracked a small smile. "You never approve of anybody I date."

"What can I say? I'm your overprotective brother," I said and she laughed. "At least you're getting Jerry off your case, right?"

"And Daddy." She shook her head. "Hasn't Jerry been with anybody else?"

"Of course he has," I said, folding my arms. "I don't know what his problem is. But he's been hung up on you for a long time."

"You know how it is with those kind of guys. All alpha because I called it quits," she said. "Wanting what he can't have."

My eyes darted straight over to Dean whose face was lit up with a grin for Billie and something in my heart surged. Billie had invited his close friend, Leo, from school and he looked content. They would probably head inside to play video games soon enough.

Why couldn't life be as easy as that?

Cassie and Grammy got the bride and groom and their

parents set up in the cabin while we finished making the yard look presentable.

In the afternoon the guests ate sandwiches for lunch on some tables and chairs we had set up near the main house and played some horseshoe and corn hole in the yard. I had handcrafted those angled boards, Billie painted them with Yankees colors, and Grammy had sewn the bean bags, so I was glad to see they were finally getting more use.

I watched as Dean interacted with the guests and each time he held Cassie's hand or put his arm around her, I felt a swell of longing. Wishing I could be the stand-in and that kind of thinking would get me nowhere fast.

Jerry, who had shown up to drop off some baked goods from Mrs. Lorrigan, was sulking and so was my brother Braden as his girlfriend followed him around. Guess we were all suffering in one way or another.

My dad had never remarried after my mother died and I wondered if he felt like she could never be replaced. Grammy was the rock of this family, and as usual was chatting with everybody and surrounded by a group of well-wishers.

Sometimes I tried to picture the future but it was hard to envision. Would I become my dad in twenty years' time? Or maybe it would only be Billie and me. But that couldn't be accurate. Billie had the right to marry somebody he loved.

More than likely, I'd always be alone.

17

CALLUM

After lunch, everybody seemed to retreat to their own rooms to prepare for the rehearsal dinner. The bridesmaids and groomsmen would be arriving for the meal. We didn't have the space to house everybody, so most guests were staying at the motel in town.

The wedding would take place in the field behind the small orchard and it was definitely an appealing view. Thankfully my cousin had hired her own catering company. No way my grandmother could keep up with that much food for the reception tomorrow. Not even with Billie's help. But she insisted on cooking for the celebration tonight and had planned a simple menu weeks ago.

Grammy was busy in the kitchen with Cassie and Billie, who had just pulled out a tray from the oven. He loved baking most of all and if his dessert wasn't for after dinner, I'd have reached for a warm chocolate chip cookie based on that smell alone.

Billie's guest, Leo, sat peeling potatoes at the table with Bullseye beneath his legs. He was a good friend but it was still surprising to see a kid his age not grumbling about being put to work. The Xbox had been abandoned in the next room, so they must've taken a break to help.

I wondered where Dean had wandered off to but then remembered how he'd offered to assist Braden in picking up additional bottles of wine for the party.

"Come and see me, Callum," my father's voice sounded from the hall.

I stepped inside the office, which was a large room off the kitchen. We all shared this space from time to time, but I had all but claimed it years ago. "Something up, Daddy?"

"Just looking over some bills," he said, with a stack of envelopes in front of him. "What groups have you reserved for the next couple of months?"

I sat down in the seat across from him, my fingers itching to get to that computer screen so I could tell him exactly what we had planned here on the preserve. But I wasn't going to kick my own father out of my chair. Truth be told, it was one of the only places I felt I truly belonged, outside of the sawmill. And for that I was grateful, because it meant the work I did mattered. At least in some regard.

"We're booked most weeks with one group or another," I said, leaving off the fact that a couple of our regulars had recently cancelled. "I left that last week of August open to prepare for the alligator hunt next door."

He was constantly stressed this time of year, afraid we'd soon be living off of crumbs. But we always made do. I could definitely finish the Adirondack chairs I'd begun working on in the spring and sell them for a decent price at my aunt's shop. Or we could place another ad in the Gainesville newspaper to attract new customers. I'd figure out a way to keep us afloat.

"Glad to hear it. Keep up the good work." He arched his back trying to stretch out his spasm. I've seen the same look on his face too many times to count in the past few months.

"Getting worse?" I stood up and approached him, placing my hand on his shoulder.

"A bit," he said. "No worries, I've got a doc appointment in town next week, might increase the meds."

All that information did was reinforce the fact that he needed me here more than ever. I placed my fingers on his back and attempted to get out the kink. "Hold still. Might do you good to see a masseuse."

"All I need is to add more bills," he said, groaning as I dug my thumbs beneath his shoulder blades.

"Consider it physical therapy. Your doctor should be able to make you a referral so that it's covered under our insurance," I said, when his head dipped down as I massaged the muscle.

"Might be possible," he said and then straightened himself. Discussion over.

He opened more mail and I wanted to warn him not to mix up my carefully laid piles or he'd make more work for me.

"So what's your opinion on Dean?" he asked absently, while he studied some line items on the gas bill.

My entire body stiffened and I backed away to sit down in the chair.

"What does it matter?" I said, hoping for a change in subject. "I'm not sure they're all that serious. Cassie hasn't said so, at least."

"Billie's certainly taken to him. Seems like a solid guy, is all," he said. "If not a bit too polished around the edges. Not like Jerry. Jerry would've—"

"She doesn't want to be with Jerry and you know you can't force it," I said. "You've got to give it up."

He adjusted himself against the seat and sighed. "I know, I was just hoping..."

"Shouldn't her happiness matter more?" I asked, my hands clenching into fists. "Can't help Mr. Lorrigan is being a stubborn old coot about merging our land."

"But joining with him would give us the security we need," he said. "I'm not getting any younger."

"And you've got four children who will help out in one way or another," I said. "Braden favors you. He was made for this land."

As he stared at me I could see the question hanging from his lips. *What about you?*

But I think he was terrified to ask it. He knew that I loved this property and my family, but something was off when it came to me. I suspect we'd continue to avoid the subject for years to come. Unless I just came clean.

I imagined saying the words out loud right in that instant. *Dad, I'm gay. And I think Mr. Lorrigan suspects it.*

But as I noticed the latest worry lines that had formed around his eyes along with a new crop of gray hair at his temple, I realized this was not the time. Maybe at the end of gator season, when he was more relaxed about our finances. Maybe by then I will have stopped reliving those couple of stolen moments with Dean. Imagining what could've been.

"We're going to make do without them," I said, in a strong and steady voice. "We don't need anybody else. It'll be better that way."

"You're right, you know," he said, stretching his neck. "You've always had better business sense. Able to see the big picture."

I stood up, unsure of whether his view of me was accurate or not. "Just let it be, Daddy. Enjoy having Cassie around."

18

DEAN

The rest of the day went by in a blur. The rehearsal dinner was filled with laughter, good food, and plenty of reminiscing with the relatives. I learned a ton about the Montgomery family, in particular that they weren't so conventional all the time. Apparently, Cassie's mom was a pistol when it came to subjects she was passionate about, challenging the local church minister on a couple of issues. Maybe she knew that her children would one day need a resilient voice.

It seemed Cassie had grown into her mother's likeness, something she should've taken pride in. I think she had her grammy to thank for those solid genes as well.

Braden's girlfriend had also arrived and she seemed more animated about the state of their relationship than he was. Not that he treated her badly, just that there was some enthusiasm that appeared to be lacking. In fact, he seemed to be sulking.

Leo had already gone home but his friendship with Billie had left me curious about so many things when it came to the youngest Montgomery's life. I felt relieved that he had a good buddy—one who accepted him no less. It was tough enough being a teenager. But an adolescent with disabilities would be tenfold.

Over the course of the night, plenty of relatives had asked Cassie and me questions about the state of our relationship and I could feel Callum's gaze on me the entire time. But this wasn't the same kind of scrutiny I felt from him the first day I arrived. It now seemed something altogether different. More like attentiveness. Laced with rigidity.

I couldn't imagine it would be jealousy. Cassie and I were playing a role after all. But maybe that's where the envy cut deep. The fact that we could be out in the open, pretending or not.

After the rehearsal dinner and plenty of bottles of wine, everybody retired to bed. Grammy handed Callum an armload of extra towels to walk over to the cabin for an additional guest, and I sat down on the porch swing to wait for him. I had felt so restless all night, almost agitated, wanting so badly to touch him again.

I hopped off the bench as soon as I saw him approaching the house, my fingers rubbing along the white paint finish on one of the pristine Adirondack chairs.

"Did you make all of this furniture as well?" I asked, suddenly curious about the information Cassie had shared earlier about Callum enjoying the sawmill and workshop they had built on their property.

"I did," he said, his eyes wide and round. "I paint the chairs different colors and sell them in town. They go for a pretty penny and can be in high demand."

"Nice craftsmanship," I said, taking in the slats and rounded corners. "And really cool."

"Thanks," Callum said, as a smile indented his cheek. "What are you doing out here? I thought you'd be in bed."

"Waiting on you." I lowered my voice, looking toward the front door to make sure that we were in fact alone.

Callum worried his bottom lip through his teeth, as if unsure of my intentions.

"I'm going to skip my run in the morning," I said, but it was only in an effort to fill in the dead air. "And will help any way I can with the wedding prep."

He nodded, holding my gaze. "Is anybody awake in the house?"

"Not sure," I said, as he moved closer. "Don't think so. I just need…"

"Me too," he said so low I could barely hear him. His voice was throaty and pained, as if he were only holding on to a thin measure of control. "It's too risky out here."

"I know," I said, disappointment settling in my chest. "I'll just see you in the—"

"Have you ever seen a peacock up close?" he asked all at once, cutting off my train of thought. He had also spoken in a normal tone, which told me this information was safe for any listening ears.

"I don't think so," I said, whipping my head around the property as if I'd see one walking up. "Why?"

"Sometimes Gus comes out at night," he said, swinging his arm behind him. "It's a misconception that peacocks are nocturnal, but he seems to be."

"Gus?" I said, biting back a laugh.

"Yup, Billie named him," he said, smiling. "Best part? He's albino."

"There are albino peacocks?" I asked. "Are you just messing with me again? Like how you told me to clap loud that first day to fend off rattlesnakes?"

His eyebrow quirked up as if considering what I'd said. "That was valid information I gave you. And if you don't believe me about albino peacocks, then follow me."

I sprang off the porch and trailed him down the stairs. We strode side-by-side, away from the running path, and I ached to reach for his hand. Callum led me beyond the orchard, where the ceremony would take place. The white tent, arch, and wooden chairs with neatly tied silk bows gleamed in the moonlight.

"Looks really pretty out here tonight," I said, motioning toward the decorations. "Peaceful, too."

"Sure does," he said, walking past the two alabaster columns. "Gus would fit right in, if only he'd show himself during the day. My cousin would love that. Could walk down the aisle with her."

"What do you mean?" I asked.

"Shhh..." he said, stopping near a small grassy meadow. "Come over here so he doesn't spot us."

We tiptoed quietly behind a large oak tree and watched the pasture as if we were nighttime hunters. At least that's what it felt like. Or maybe birdwatchers would be a more accurate description.

I was standing in front of Callum as he pointed over my shoulder, when suddenly he wrapped his large arm around my torso and yanked me against him. It felt so good to have my body resting against his that I bit back a moan. Being out here with him in the dark under the moon and the dense canopy of the tree, felt like we were enclosed in our own little sanctuary. I relaxed into his embrace and sighed.

"You see him?" he whispered against my ear and I couldn't help shivering.

Strutting into the middle of the field was Gus and I could hear our soft breaths panting in unison as we attempted to keep quiet. I'd stay silent in his arms all night long if I could.

Gus paced around in circles as if feeling out the joint before he came to a halt and fanned open his magnificent snowy feathers. He took a few steps closer in the grass, walking in what could only be described as a swagger. I had never seen anything like it.

"Whoa," I said in awe. "That is spectacular."

"Right?" he murmured against my hair and I could feel the vibration of his voice thrumming in my bones. "It's like this is the only time he feels safe enough to let it all hang out. Guess I can understand that bird on some base level."

I looked up at him right then and our eyes locked. Callum leaned forward, cupping my jaw with his coarse fingers and kissing me with a heartbreaking tenderness he hadn't before. And it nearly did me in, as a rush of emotions crammed my chest along with molten desire.

His tongue slid gently against mine as his finger brushed lightly across my cheek. It was so sexy and shuddery that I nearly crumpled to my knees.

Callum grabbed a firm hold of my biceps and flipped me so that I was flush against the tree trunk, my hands blindly groping for him. My longing had reached its peak and I needed him in the worst way, in any manner he'd give himself to me.

"Please," I ground out. I didn't know exactly what I was asking for, but somehow he knew because his lips became firmer, his tongue explored deeper, making me lose all manner of breathing. I was blinded by how much I wanted him in that moment, praying for more than the stolen five minutes we'd been offered earlier.

Callum sank his body solidly against mine and when our groins pressed together, both of us moaned.

His fingers fumbled to unbutton my pants, warring with mine, as I attempted to do the same. Our mouths still fused together, we frantically reached for each other's cocks, pumping wildly, our kisses becoming even more reckless.

"I won't last long," he grunted. He slid his thumb over my head, circling the underside of my length, which felt so sensitive to his touch, I was ready to detonate.

"Me neither," I said, fisting his thick cock more solidly and pumping him up and down.

Keeping our eyes open, our tongues met in a delicate dance as we thrust into each other's hands propelling ourselves into oblivion.

He shot off first, groaning against my mouth. "Fucking hell."

As I captured his sounds, my entire body shuddered and I came in spurting ribbons of come all over his hand and wrist. He kept clutching me while I got my breathing under control, my fingers finally releasing his cock.

I watched as he tugged his hand away, my seed captured in his fist. He reached down and mixed my come with his by rubbing it into his groin, right above that downy patch of hair. As if he wanted me to be absorbed into his skin.

No lover had ever done something like that and it was so damn sexy, it nearly made me stiff again.

His come was still dripping from my hand, so I reached up and thrust a finger inside my mouth. "Mmmmm..."

"Holy fuck," he groaned and then slammed his mouth over mine, his tongue reaching deep, tasting himself on me. Damn, if I didn't wish we had been somewhere more private in that moment.

We were covered in come and sweat and were breathing hard. I looked over Callum's shoulder and barked out a laugh.

"What?" he asked, amusement in his voice.

"We just gave Gus a show," I said, grinning.

Gus was frozen in place staring in our direction.

"Well, we had to repay the favor," Callum said, smiling, his eyes still blissed out from his orgasm.

We watched as Gus folded his feathers against his body and wandered off into the woods.

Using the bottom of our shirts to clean up, we tucked ourselves back in place. It was sticky and messy but I didn't even care because it was Callum's come on me.

I stretched forward to give him a quick peck, but our lips lingered and held and we ended up making out for several more minutes against that tree.

"I want to stay out here with you all night," I said, dragging my mouth away.

"Damn. If only we could make that happen," he whispered against my lips.

When we heard a twig snap we pulled apart as if we'd been caught.

My heart was beating wildly hoping one of our wedding guests hadn't wandered out here.

But it was only a couple of deer at the edge of the woods, intently watching us.

"Well look at that," I said in a wistful voice. "Not something you see every day in the city."

So common in these parts, it was likely no longer wondrous nor appreciated—kind of like walking out of your apartment building and finding a Starbucks on every corner.

Wouldn't it be something to have Callum discover those things for himself the first time in my neighborhood? I shook that impossible thought from my head.

"You head back first," Callum said, kissing the side of my head one last time. "I'm right behind you."

19

DEAN

After the ceremony, which was really nice in a country elegant sort of way, the reception began. The bride, who had been barefoot walking down the aisle, now wore some white rubber flip-flops. The groom took off his coat and bolero tie. It was casual in a way that I would appreciate at my own nuptials someday. The setting was perfect in my opinion. What could be better than being surrounded by family and friends?

I tried to picture Cassie having her own wedding here on the preserve and during the service, I couldn't keep my gaze from wandering over to Callum who seemed to listen intently to the couple as they read their own vows.

The bridal party took photos in the orchard and dinner was served shortly thereafter. We sat at a table with other family members from the area and it felt like being studied beneath a microscope. Given Cassie's tight set jaw, she was already beginning to tire of questions about the status of our relationship. So placing my arm behind her chair had been the most affection I'd shown her tonight.

Callum was sitting beside Grammy at the next table over, and

I noticed how in tune he seemed when our conversation bled into questions about the city Cassie and I lived. I wondered if he'd ever have any desire to visit.

As soon as the music began from the middle of the field where a deejay had set up shop, the tables cleared, and everybody seemed to be getting their groove on. I danced two slow songs with Cassie for appearances sake, while Jerry fumed from his table in the corner. But there were plenty of single ladies here and I had to wonder what his deal was. He couldn't possibly believe he and Cassie had anything in common—they seemed different as chalk and cheese.

"I'm surprised Jerry hasn't busted in on me yet," I said, looking over her shoulder. Jerry's eyes were on us, but also on a couple of bridesmaids nearby. One of them had bent over to speak to him and I noticed how his gaze kept darting to her ample cleavage.

"God, I hope not," Cassie said as I twirled her around in her pretty yellow sundress. "But I'd sure like to strike up a conversation with an old classmate I see over there."

"Where?" I asked, craning my neck.

"Don't be so obvious," she said, firmly squeezing my arm. "He's at the table next to my dad's."

There was a guy seated will a full head of blond waves and what appeared to be a nice physique. When I made eye contact with him, he looked away.

"He's pretty cute," I said, wiggling my eyebrows. "He keeps looking this way."

"He didn't used to have all of that gorgeous hair. He kept it pretty short," she said. "In school, Dermot was extremely shy and pretty nerdy."

"Nothing wrong with nerds," I said. "Especially if they're as fine as him."

She thumped me on the shoulder and rolled her eyes.

"You should go talk to him, play catch up," I said, looking over at him again. "He's sitting beside somebody. Is that his date?"

"Good question," she said, scrunching up her nose. "Just keep dancing until I figure out what to say to him."

We swayed back and forth as I watched my good friend transform into some shy schoolgirl right before my eyes. It was endearing in a lot of ways because she was always busting my balls about one thing or another.

She was different around her family, though, and maybe that was why she needed to get away, to spread her wings a bit more. She definitely had competition from some strong personalities in the Montgomery family.

"The night's almost over," I said as we moved in circles. "I think we pulled it off."

"Thank God," she said. "No offense, but I don't want to be your girlfriend any more. Though I'm still really glad you came."

"Likewise," I said, laughing. "I was going to break up with you tomorrow anyway. Especially since you're about to cheat on me with Dermot."

After the music changed, I finally made my way over to Callum who had an empty seat beside him at the table. I figured this was a safe time to approach him. I wouldn't have many more chances and that made melancholy sit heavy in my gut.

He looked so damn good in that gray suit and bright blue tie, I could've eaten him with a spoon.

"You clean up nice," I said, low enough so only he could hear.

"You do as well." His eyes flared and his voice was thick. "Wouldn't mind getting you alone. I'd like you naked with only your glasses and that striped tie."

"Glasses?" I could feel my face flush. "The ones I use for reading?"

"They're hot as fuck," he murmured in my direction.

"You can't say things like that to me in public." I adjusted myself on the seat, dying to touch him. What I wouldn't give to pull him out on the dance floor and slide my body next to his. Hold him, kiss him, feel his strong embrace.

"So, um, did you have enough to eat?" he asked. I expected to find a smirk on his face but instead there was genuine concern.

"I ate the pasta and vegetables. Left the venison," I said practically shivering at the thought.

"I'm not a fan of gamey meat either," he said, shrugging. "So I ate the same as you."

"Aha, a closeted vegetarian." One of my eyebrows quirked and he shook his head, amused. "What about rattlesnake jerky?"

I thought back to that first day I met him. How strong and confident he looked in the face of that serpent.

"It sells well around here." Callum shrugged. "We do what we can to stay afloat."

That statement made me realize how indebted to the family business Callum must've felt. I wanted to talk more about it, ask him his real thoughts about all of this. About everything, really. He was one of the most interesting men I'd ever had the pleasure of meeting. I wouldn't have said the same a few days ago.

20

DEAN

When I next looked across the tabletops, the crowd seemed to be thinning out. The bride and groom were making their rounds to talk to their remaining guests, some of whom they probably hadn't seen in a long while. Billie was beside Leo, who had arrived for the ceremony with his parents. Dermot and Cassie were talking and laughing, and by the looks of it, were now standing up to dance.

"I think Cassie is happy to see Dermot," I said in a conspiratorial whisper.

"Dermot's a good guy," Callum said, watching them walk to the middle of the floor. "His family owns an orchard and he runs one of their roadside stands."

"Nice," I said, admiring his tall physique. Cassie's modesty with him on the dance floor amused me. "Though, if Cassie spends the rest of the night talking to Dermot, our rouse is over."

"What do you mean?" Callum asked, looking from my eyes to my lips and back again. I was liable to jump him any second now.

"She might have to fess up that we're only friends," I said, knocking my foot against his beneath the table. "Your dad or

Grammy might get suspicious. They'll wonder why she's not devoting more time to me."

"True," he said, a line of worry wrinkling his forehead. "But you can always make something up. Worked for me for years. I've been in the closet so long, it's hard to even see the light on the other side of the door."

"I understand," I said, my heart squeezing for him. "I have a friend back home who joined a religious ministry to please his family. It's painful to watch him ignore the best parts of himself."

"How long have you been out?" His tone was serious, his eyes searching.

"Since I was a teen. After my brother died...like I said on our run, I just needed to be true to myself," I said. "My parents still don't talk about it. Like they think it'll go away."

"At least you were brave," he said looking slightly green. "I didn't realize I was gay until I was nearly an adult and look at me. I'm still hiding."

"I think it depends on your circumstances. If it doesn't fair well for your personal or financial safety, that's something to consider," I said, having heard one too many stories about friends who were kicked out on the street or lost their jobs. "I'm free, sure. Even if somebody doesn't want anything to do with me. But I live in a different place than here."

"I should at least open up to somebody who cares about me." A flash of pain crossed his features. "I've decided to tell Cassie."

"Sounds good. You need an ally in your family." I looked over to Leo's family's table, where Billie and his friend sat conspiring about something. "And Billie is going to need one too."

"Billie?" He stared hard at his brother as he sat near Leo, his innocent eyelashes fluttering, and realization dawned on him. "He tell you that?"

"No," I said. "But it seems obvious to me. It's only a matter of time before he needs a release, an outlet, somebody to share things with."

"Fuck, my father is going to have a heart attack," Callum said, his lips twisting into a distorted smile. "Two in one family."

"Happens more that you would think," I said, rushing my fingers through my hair. "DNA is like that."

"Thing is," Callum said, after chugging back his beer. "Billie would be the braver one and that's just pathetic."

Cassie was helping pass a tray around with wedding cake and as she approached, I reached for a couple of slices, placing one of the plates in front of Callum.

I winked at Cassie as we ate the sweet confection and watched as she offered Dermot and his date some slices as well. I noticed how she purposely skipped Jerry's table and made her way to Grammy, where she sat with some older family members and the aunt who owned the furniture store in town that Callum talked about.

Callum's gaze darted around the dance floor before landing on Jerry who was talking to the bridesmaid from earlier at his table. They looked pretty cozy now.

"Mr. Lorrigan knows," Callum said motioning with his head in the family's direction. "About me."

I sat up straighter as Mr. Lorrigan narrowed his eyes in Callum's direction. "What do you mean?"

"He saw me in town with Jason last year and since then he's been treating me different," he said in a lower register. "I figure he doesn't want to merge our land if a faggot is involved in the business."

I cringed at the use of that word, but he had made his point. "What exactly was it that you were doing in town?"

"Jason and I were coming out of a hotel room together," he said. "The messed-up thing about it was that Mr. Lorrigan was as well—with another woman. Motherfucker."

I wanted to march over to Mr. Lorrigan and slap the shit out of him. "So it's okay to cheat on your wife but not okay to be gay?"

"Exactly," he said. "What he doesn't realize is that I could hurt him as well. He thinks what he's got on me is worse than what I got on him? Fuck that."

"That's what makes me most livid," I said, tugging at my tie. It had suddenly become too constricting. "People's fucked-up logic."

"If I come out, he's got nothing to hold over my head anymore. We'll lose business, which will kill my dad," he said, shaking his head. "But Mr. Lorrigan's marriage would be in jeopardy."

We sat silently fuming and in that moment, I felt even more connected to Callum. He had shared something personal and I was grateful for his trust in me. It made leaving tomorrow afternoon that much more bittersweet.

"How do you think your dad would take the news about Billie?" I asked as the two boys ate cake and laughed, their eyes flirting. Young love was so fragile as it was.

"I think he'd eventually accept the idea," he said. "He'd be sad, though, wondering if Billie will find happiness. He already worries about that."

"Wouldn't he feel the same about you?" I asked.

"I don't know. It's hard to disappoint him." His mouth drew into a tight line. "He was so shattered when my mother died. All I've wanted to do was help him keep his legacy for this family."

I thought about my own family. How my brother was dead and my father would have no heir and that same familiar guilt washed over me. Guess we'd always disappoint our parents in some way or another. But I could only live for me. It was exhausting constantly trying to please somebody else. Especially if they didn't appreciate all the unique things about you in the first place.

I unfastened the top button of my dress shirt and loosened my tie, figuring it didn't matter this late in the evening if I was dressed perfectly or not. Callum's heated gaze followed my fingers.

"What?" I said, my throat suddenly dry.

"I just want to kiss you again," he said. "So damn bad."

"The feeling's mutual," I said, meeting his eyes. His red brown hair was brushed back from his forehead. He looked so handsome. "In a lot of ways I wish your lips weren't so addictive."

He smirked. "Why is that?"

"Because I'll be leaving soon," I said, nearly breathless at the thought. "And I'll have too much time on my trip home to think about that mouth."

He looked slightly crestfallen and I realized that this conversation was probably way too heavy for only knowing somebody for a few days. So why did it feel like so much longer?

"Callum," Grammy said, interrupting our conversation. I was so lost in Callum's gaze that I didn't even see her walk up. Fuck. She stood in front of us in her beaded dress, looking more like high society than country grandmother. "We're going to need more booze. Your cousins are going to drink us into the ground."

"There's an extra case that Braden stored in the kitchen pantry just in case," I said, having witnessed him stashing it after our alcohol run.

"I'll get it," Callum stood up.

"Maybe Dean feels like helping you," Grammy said. "He must be bored out of his mind at this event."

I looked over at Cassie who was back to catching up with Dermot at his table. Grammy followed my line of sight and all I could think was that she knew—somehow she knew—that Cassie and I weren't really together.

"Not at all," I said. "Your family is great. But I can definitely help Callum."

Grammy smiled, and I detected a wicked glint in her eyes.

21

CALLUM

Fuck, Dean was messing with my head. I was already hard from him talking about kissing me. But there was definitely another layer of depth between us as well, after our serious discussion about coming out. I had shared something with him that I hadn't told anybody other than Jason and I had no earthly idea why, except maybe that I trusted him after such a short period of time.

He walked unassumingly beside me back to the house, and it was as if we couldn't do or say anything to draw attention to ourselves. Away from the noise of the music and reception, it was strangely serene back here. My ears were ringing simply from the lack of noise.

My heart hammered as Dean's hand brushed innocently against mine. Damn, I wanted to grab him and kiss him senseless, the way we did last night against that oak tree. We walked up the steps and into the kitchen. I opened the creaky pantry door and tugged on the light that hung from a string. It was a decent sized room, much like a closet, and it held all of our extra food supplies. If the apocalypse ever came, this family would be set.

I spotted the box of liquor on the floor as the pantry door creaked closed behind Dean.

Breathing heavily, we stared each other down, the air growing positively electric. I didn't know who stepped forward first but suddenly we were toe to toe sharing the same air.

"Dean," I said. "Fuck."

"Don't think," he whispered as his fingers wrapped around my neck and his soft lips brushed over mine. "Just feel."

I moaned at the taste of him. As his tongue entered my mouth, I wanted to stand there the rest of the night just like that, kissing him. His fingers traced down my collarbone to my chest and brushed over my nipples. I hissed from the contact.

He drew his mouth away. "Are you sensitive here?"

"God, yeah," I said, as he rubbed his knuckles over my nipples again. "Always have been."

And then his fingers were loosening my tie. Dean swung the long strand of blue material over my neck and unfastened the top few buttons, exposing my chest. I considered that somebody could walk into the house at any second but found I didn't even care, not when his hands were on me.

His tongue feathered across my nipples over and over again and I moaned as my head sank back against the shelf of canned goods. Nobody had paid this much attention to my chest before. My cock, sure. But this was heaven.

"You *are* sensitive," he grunted out. "Damn, I love that."

When he sucked on one of the hardened pebbles, I gasped, and nearly came in my pants. I reached down to adjust myself but he swatted my hand away. "I'm about to make a mess."

"Tell me when you're close," he said, his eyes meeting mine. "Got it?"

Fuck, he was going to have to pull off and then I'd be walking around with blue balls all night.

He palmed my rigid cock through my pants and I thrust into

his hand, my fingers digging into the edge of the shelf to steady myself.

"Got it?" he asked again, switching to my other nipple, and I could hardly think straight.

"Yeah, okay," I said, so blissed out I would agree to anything at that point.

As his tongue continued to lick, bite, and suck my nipples, I skated dangerously close to the edge. His mouth traveled a couple of inches upward and his lips closed tightly around the skin. My hands braced his head, my fingers tightening in his thick hair. When his mouth popped off, he'd left a substantial mark. "That's so you remember me being here."

"You think I'd ever fucking forget?" I groaned low and throaty, the familiar heat licking down my spine and drawing my balls up tight. "Oh God, I'm going to come. So close…"

He kept sucking while his hands worked swiftly to unclasp my belt and unzip my pants.

"Damn, that is one nice cock," he said, holding my shaft in his fist as he knelt down and ran his tongue over the slit. My back arched as I propelled my length toward his wet and inviting lips, begging for more. "I want you to come in my mouth. I can't wait to taste you."

Before I could register his words, he closed his lips over my head and sucked me into his warm heat, while his fingertips simultaneously clamped down on my nipples. All of the different sensations were too much to bear at once and I groaned loud and long, shooting my seed down his throat.

My knees trembling, my knuckles white from my grip on the shelf behind me, he cleaned up every last drop and continued laving my softened cock until I nudged his face away.

He drew his lips from my dick and looked up at me, his eyes glazed over with lust. His thumb swiped at the corner of his mouth as he hummed.

I yanked him to his feet and kissed him, my tongue digging

deep in his mouth, unwilling to let him go right then. After a minute more, he pulled back and helped get my clothes back in place.

"Now I'll taste you in my mouth the rest of the night," he said over his shoulder as he pushed through the door and strode ahead of me, maybe to give himself a chance to cool off.

I stood there breathing heavily and marveling at the fact that I just got sucked off in my own kitchen pantry with my family a few hundred feet outside. Fuck, I had never been that careless before. But damn, I couldn't say I regretted even one second of it.

As I lifted the case of wine I thought about how I needed more of Dean. I didn't want him to leave without getting a taste of him too. He had just made me come from nipple stimulation alone and that made my cheeks flame hot.

When I got back to the reception, Dean was sitting beside Cassie and sipping from a bottle of beer. I thought of the fact that he would have to continue pretending to be her date for the remainder of his hours here, might even hold her hand a few times more. The idea of him touching somebody else after he'd just been with me, made my stomach turn.

I knew then that I would tell Cassie first thing in the morning.

Dean barely made eye contact with me the rest of the night and that did not sit well. I found I needed his warm and intense gaze, at least for one more day. So that I knew for certain he wanted me as plainly as I wanted him.

Though it didn't make a lick of sense, no way I wanted him to leave without at least knowing one thing. That we'd have given whatever this was between us a decent shot, if we could've had it any other way.

22

DEAN

I t was difficult not to stare at Callum as I sat at a table beside Cassie. But I knew as soon as I made eye contact, and saw his tie slightly askew, I would be hard as a fence post again and I needed to keep my longing for him in check.

Damn, he'd been so responsive to nipple stimulation. I didn't know many guys who were that sensitive and it was fucking hot. To be able to put my mouth on his cock and taste his come did things to me as well. I wished we had been alone in his room so I could've kept going, had him all to myself for longer.

"So tell me about Dermot," I said to Cassie, who had a distracted glaze to her eyes.

"He...we..." she said in a flustered voice that I'd only heard early on in the year when she'd been crushing hard on her professor.

"Whoa," I said, trying to keep my humor in check. "You like him."

"Stop," she said, color rising in her cheeks. "We were always friends in school. Just lost touch in recent years."

My gaze swung across the grassy field to check out Dermot more carefully. He was broad shouldered with nice blond hair and dark eyes. "Well he's certainly changed if your reaction to him is any indication."

"You've got that right," she said in a wistful voice. My friend was definitely smitten.

"Does he think you're here with me?" I asked, low in her ear.

She chewed her lip. "I kind of told him that we were only platonic. He brought a friend to the reception as well."

"So you can tell him about us but not your family?" I said, in mock outrage.

"My family is different," she scoffed. "You can see that for yourself."

"I'm only teasing you," I said, hoping like hell she and Callum talked soon. "But I'm starting to think that you would've been fine this week without me. Outside of Jerry trailing along behind you every chance he got."

"Exactly," she said. "So my plan worked, even if I pretended in front of my family as well. Eventually I'll tell them something."

The bride was tipsy and swaying in her wedding dress on the dance floor. Earlier she had been dirty dancing with the groom. Everybody seemed to be having a good time, even Mr. Montgomery, who had been sitting at a table with distant relatives.

Having a celebration beneath the full moon and luminescent stars was enchanting, actually. Thankfully, the Lorrigans had just left, Jerry giving Cassie a final glance, as her shoulders noticeably relaxed.

"Seems like the party is wrapping up," I said. "Maybe you should get in a final dance with Dermot."

"We'll see," she said, bumping my shoulder and dipping her head. "Looks like you and Callum have become friends."

I tried to remain neutral, keeping my lips in a neat line. "Guess so."

I'd breathe a sigh of relief when it was all out in the open. I was liable to become a big fat lust-starved mess in another hour.

Just then Dermot approached our table and introduced

himself to me. I wanted to give them some privacy so after a couple minutes, I stood up and headed to the bar.

I fell into a conversation with a couple of uncles and then Cassie's father approached me.

"Where did my daughter wander off to?" he asked and my head snapped toward the table we had just vacated. Shit, they were no longer there.

"She was catching up with old friends," I said, attempting to cover up my own surprise. "Thank you for having me here, sir."

"You're welcome to stay as long as you like," he said, patting my shoulder and drifting off to talk to more relatives.

I wasn't sure he'd say that if he knew that I'd just gotten his son off in the kitchen pantry.

Callum was busy with a couple of female guests who had cornered him into a conversation. I imagined he was considered quite the catch in this town. But even I could tell that there was a vibe he personified to ward people off. Like lightning crackling just beneath the surface of his skin. You got too close, he just might strike. Or run. Either one wasn't ideal.

Eventually, I had decided I was tired and ready for some solitude and quiet. I trudged back to the house, sank down on the steps, and looked over the Montgomery property. It truly was picturesque. I had definitely underestimated a great deal.

This was a hardworking family steeped in long-standing relationships and tradition. They had lost the matriarch early, but two other strong women had stepped up to the plate.

Right then I felt a deep pang in my stomach about my own brother, Shawn, and my less than desirable relationship with my parents.

Billie walked up the drive with Bullseye, a glimmer of a smile on his face, maybe happy with how his own night had gone. I wondered what Shawn would've confided in me about his own emotions and connections if he were still alive.

"Is something wrong?" Billie asked as he sat down beside me.

"Not really," I said, bumping his knee playfully. "Just thinking."

"About what?" he asked, as Bullseye settled in beside him.

"About my brother, Shawn," I said, with a dejected smile. "In some ways you remind me of him."

"I do?" he asked, his eyebrows arching. "Did something happen to him?"

"He died of cancer a few years ago," I said. "But I'll always remember how sweet and brave he was. That's how you remind me of him, because you have those qualities too."

His face went through a series of emotions, from glum to surprise to pride. But I didn't want to spoil the mood, so it was time to change the subject.

"Tell me about Leo," I said. "You guys hang out a lot?"

"He's a good friend." He kept his eyes averted and his cheeks darkened with a wash of color. "His parents know my cousin, that's why they were at the wedding."

"Want to talk about it?" I said in a measured voice, not sure if I should be crossing the line. But somehow with Billie, I just knew I could reach out. We already shared a connection from hanging out the past couple of days.

He was stroking Bullseye's coat, when he mumbled, "About what?"

"Maybe I'm wrong but…" I took a fortifying breath. "You have a crush on him."

His eyes widened and he looked around like his dad or Grammy might come charging out at any instant.

"Don't worry, your secret is completely safe with me," I said in a lower voice, even though I was pretty certain nobody else was nearby. "It's got to be hard not to have anybody to talk to about it."

"I just…I…yeah." He merely stared at me, at a loss for words. As if I'd just told him I'd discovered a buried treasure beneath the house or something.

"Does he feel the same way?" I asked, to assist in moving him along and hopefully to help him not feel so awkward.

He watched me through lowered lashes and nodded. I assumed as much based on the subtle looks passed between them.

"Have you guys...?" I asked.

He shook his head, biting his lip. "He holds my hand when nobody else is around."

"Anything else?" I asked and suddenly felt terrible that he didn't have somebody to help him navigate through all of these emotions.

"No way," he responded immediately, which told me that this was perhaps new for the both of them and it was probably best to keep it simple. At least for now.

I placed my hand on his shoulder. "You can always talk to me. I'll give you my number."

"You will?" he said and his eyes looked shiny right then as if grateful for my support. "How long are you staying? I like having you around."

"That means a lot." My smile faltered a bit. "I planned on leaving tomorrow afternoon. Cassie will be here a couple weeks longer. But I've got to head back soon."

"Can't you stay a couple more days?" he asked in a pleading tone. "There's a huge carnival in town and fireworks. Shady Pines has a booth there and it's a ton of fun."

Something warm slid across my chest. God, I adored this kid. And truth be told, I was enjoying my time on the preserve as well. Not only because of Callum, though that definitely factored in. It was more that it was a simpler kind of life where you learned to appreciate other things besides the commotion a city brings. There was a certain kind of peace to living off the land and understanding its benefit.

"I'll see what Cassie says," I said, figuring she and I would be having a more serious conversation sometime soon and I had no idea what she might say to me about her brother. Would the idea totally creep her out? Shit, I hadn't thought it all the way through. I was supposed to be here as her fake boyfriend and there I was giving her brother head in a pantry.

Not that she would ever know the lurid details, but I hadn't truly considered her feelings in all of this. What if she wasn't cool with the idea of her brother and her roommate hooking up?

But in the end, what did it matter if I was taking off anyway? Maybe I should just hit the road first thing in the morning, and leave all of this behind. Eventually I'd get back in the hectic routine of my everyday life and be able to forget how Callum tasted and sounded and smelled.

"You're not really Cassie's new boyfriend, are you?" Billie's voice rang out into the night, startling me. I had been so lost in thought.

"I...no," I finally conceded. "Do you think anybody else knows?"

He looked around as he thought about it. "Not sure."

"But we're like best friends," I said, feeling the need to explain, hoping like hell he didn't accuse me of deceiving him. "Does that count?"

He smiled. "Works for me. Think I can come visit you sometime in the city?"

"Absolutely," I said, not even giving it a second thought. Though I hadn't taken Bullseye or his special needs into consideration. But he was a kid who had hopes and dreams and I'd be happy to help make it work no matter what.

"Looks like the reception is about over," I said, nodding to a couple of guests who were wandering to their cars parked on the grass. The caterer had also loaded his truck long ago. "Think anybody would notice if I slipped off to bed?"

I went back to my room, got undressed and lay in my sheets thinking long and hard about whether or not to pack up at sunrise. The thought of leaving made my chest ache.

Except it was only a week ago that I didn't even give Shady Pines Preserve a second thought. Life was funny sometimes. Sneaking up on you when you least expected it and making everything feel more exhilarating and yet heavier at the same time.

23

DEAN

I must've fallen asleep. There was a tap on my guest room door. Maybe it was Cassie telling me that she was sorry she had spent the remainder of the evening with Dermot. Hopefully nobody had questioned her about anything.

I stumbled to the door, with only the light of the moon illuminating the pathway.

After I twisted the knob there stood Callum in only a pair of sweat shorts. His chest gleamed liked he'd just finished showering.

"What time is it?" I said, rubbing my eyes.

"Late. Everybody's asleep," he whispered. "So were you. I'm sorry, I just thought—"

I wrapped my fingers around his wrist and yanked him inside.

As soon as the door closed, our bodies slammed together and we were kissing. My sluggish arms tried to reach around his neck but instead landed on his chest. My fingers splayed, I fondled the downy patch of fuzz there, and traced the purple mark I had left on him earlier. Callum's hands wound through my hair and he held me in place as his lips pummeled my mouth.

He sank to his knees and tugged at my boxers. "Callum—"

I angled my head and let out a strangled groan as his large hand fastened around my dick.

"Shhh...keep your voice down," he said, watching his fingers as they slid along my length. "All I could think about was your cock and getting my lips around it."

My dick instantly lengthened with those words.

"Look how gorgeous you are," he murmured, staring up at me. "Your hair, your lips, and those damn eyes. Deep as the sea, but always catching the light. Lose my breath every time you look my way."

Holy hot damn. Before I could respond or even form another coherent thought his lips descended downward to lick around the crown.

"Fuck." I gasped. "You make me so crazy."

My fingers shifted from his shoulders to all of that cinnamon-colored hair. It was thick and soft in my fingers and the more I tugged, the harder he sucked.

His fingers circled my balls and squeezed. My heart ricocheted against my chest as my legs began shaking. "You like that?"

"Oh God," I grunted, my vision nearly whiting out. I loved for my sac to be played with. "Yes."

His mouth moved lower to suck my balls into his mouth and lick circles around my sac. He shifted me toward the bed to give me someplace to anchor myself. The back of my thighs hit the mattress and I sank down.

Sliding more easily between my legs, he nuzzled my thighs before resuming his assault on my cock. He licked up and down my length before taking me inside all of that wet heat.

He relaxed his jaw and breathed through his nose, the cool air hitting my groin. I was so far down the back of his throat that I could feel it restricting around my head.

Humming, he continued sucking me, his tongue bathing the underside of my cock.

"You are the hottest thing I've ever seen," he said after he moved back up to my crown, tracing the ridge with his lips. "Laid out like this for me."

That did me in. Without warning, I gripped his hair, groaned loudly, and shot my load down his throat.

His eyes met mine while I shook and panted and he continued swallowing all of my come. It was so sexy to think that this giant of a man who seemed intimidating only a few days ago was now down on his knees in front of me.

I sank back on my elbows to catch my breath and he leaned over me to deliver a feathery kiss. I grabbed onto his shoulders and tugged him down to lie on top of me. His solid length ground against my bare hip. Our mouths melded together and I tasted myself on his tongue. I wished I could keep him here with me for the rest of the night and not worry that we were in his family's home.

Our legs and arms were airtight, as if we were one body, one heartbeat. We licked and nipped on each other's lips and ears and jaws. I sucked on his tongue and yanked on his hair, already hard for him again. I wanted him to fuck me straight into the mattress.

I shoved his shorts down his hips so I could feel his naked cock next to mine and he groaned as our dicks aligned. He thrust upward and rutted against me until he came all over my stomach, his mouth against my neck, capturing most of his sounds.

His lips lazily sealed around my sensitive skin and sucked. "You'll leave a mark," I groaned forcing his head back.

"Shit, I lost myself," he said, licking a stripe over where he'd sucked to soothe it. "My bad."

A noise from outside drew us out of our reverie. It might've been one of the wedding guests leaving the cabin. Hopefully not walking around in a drunken haze.

"I need to go," he said, after his gaze darted out the window.

No doubt he'd check if somebody needed assistance.

I wanted to selfishly wrap him up and keep him in my warm sheets, but I knew that I couldn't.

"I'm going to talk to Cassie in the morning," he whispered, as his pleading eyes met mine. "Will you at least stay for one more day?"

My heart lodged in my throat, I merely nodded in silent agreement. As soon as Callum lifted his body off of mine, I immediately felt the loss of his mass and heat.

Just a couple of hours ago, I considered driving off in the morning. But now that I had more of him, I was so fucked.

24

CALLUM

I sought out Cassie first thing the next morning. I wasn't sure if Dean had skipped running or not, but I was too beat after the wedding festivities, besides coming twice in one night.

Cassie was in the kitchen helping Grammy and Billie with breakfast. Billie had dark smudges beneath his eyes, but Grammy looked no worse for wear.

As I kissed her cheek, I wondered how she stayed so upbeat and strong. I honestly didn't know how we'd manage without her.

"You feeling okay, buddy?" I asked Billie as I moved around him to the coffee pot.

"Yep," he said, with a bleary smile on his face. "Don't worry, I snoozed long enough."

I knew better than to treat Billie like a fragile kid, but with his condition, it was important that he took care of himself, which included healthy eating and sleeping patterns.

"Want to take a ride to the airport with me to send off some guests?" I asked Cassie.

I couldn't bear to see Dean and Cassie pretending around me any longer, though who knew what anybody in this family believed, after she had spent half the night talking to Dermot.

Already my brain was thinking up excuses to get Dean alone and do filthy things to him. But that would only mess with my head further. Because I liked Dean, really enjoyed being around him.

Except, he lived in another state and our lives were different as night and day. Plus, I had a family business to run. So maybe this would be like getting my fill of a very sexy man until he walked out of my life. If anything, he will have been the catalyst that got Cassie and me talking again.

"Um, sure." Cassie's cheeks brightened, maybe stunned to have even been asked. "Let me get some coffee in my system."

I could see Grammy's smile in her side view. She knew Cassie and I hadn't spoken privately in years. Thankfully, she asked the question I wanted to know. "Where is your date?"

Cassie opened her mouth as if to say something, maybe confess to her relationship with Dean, but then she took a sip from her cup instead.

After swallowing, she said, "I'm pretty sure Dean's out on the trail."

"If you're still not back when Dean returns, I'll feed him and let him know where you've gone off to," Grammy said, arranging the butter on the table.

"Thanks," she said, and waited on me as I stuffed a fresh blueberry muffin in my mouth. "I'm ready when you are."

We headed out to the beat up passenger van that we mostly used for visitors and was probably in need of new tires. The guests who had early flights exited the cabin with shadows beneath their eyes and the ride to the airport was mostly silent after a hard night of celebrating.

After we dropped them off at their terminal we got back on the road.

Cassie broke the silence first. "Callum—"

"Wait, Cassie," I said, raising my hand. "Please let me say something. Or I'll chicken out again, like I have for years."

Her eyes widened in concern so I reached over and clasped her hand in reassurance. It wasn't the end of the world after all. It wasn't Mom dying and us clinging to each other again. It was just me being gay. Living in my own cage of shame and fear and it needed to stop.

She held onto my fingers and watched me expectantly.

"I know I've pulled away from you for far too long," I said, squeezing her palm. "I should've told you of all people. But, I just couldn't. I was working through it myself, and then time kept stretching out."

"Please, you're killing me," she said. "Just say it, whatever it is."

I took a deep breath. *Well here goes.* "I'm...gay."

Goddamn, to say it out loud to a family member for the first time felt...my chest was so tight and then suddenly it loosened. Some of the fear had actually drained away. It was like jumping into the lake at the beginning of the season. The water stung and then it soothed, as it surrounded you and cleansed you.

And picturing that lake got me thinking about Dean's eyes. How they were like a private spring of the warmest blue water and hurtling into them headfirst ended up saving me from myself.

I waited Cassie out as her face went through a catalogue of emotions. Shock to affection to sadness and acceptance. At least I hoped it was acceptance.

"Thanks for telling me," she said in a croaky voice. "I understand how hard that was for you. But now a lot of things are falling into place."

"Like what?" I asked, veering on the freeway to head back home.

"How you never steadily dated anybody," she said. "How you practically withdrew from everything around you."

I nodded, agreeing with her. I would shut myself in my room and only come out for chores and meals.

"You'd go into town sometimes for hours," she said, staring at the passing landscape outside her window. "I thought it was to get away, but now I'm not so sure."

I let her thought hang there. What I did in my private time might be too much to confess, even for Cassie.

"And maybe even how," she said, biting her lip. "How you were so irritated with Dean and now...now you seem to be friendly."

I almost swerved off the road. "What does Dean have to do with my confession?"

Her gaze held an apology. "Perhaps you already guessed that he and I aren't together. Maybe you know that he's my gay roommate."

"I didn't guess." I remained silent for another beat. I wasn't expecting to discuss Dean just yet. One hurdle at a time. "He told me."

She looked thunderstruck, her hand slamming over her mouth.

When her shoulders began shaking I thought I had made her cry. Just as I was about to sling an arm in her direction, she burst into laughter.

It was infectious, reminding me of how we'd try to keep it together during church services when we were younger. How Daddy would give us a stern look, but Mom would have trouble wiping away the smirk on her face as she shushed us.

"What the hell is so funny?" I asked around a smile.

"Oh, it makes so much sense now," she said, wiping at her eyes. "The way you were so pissed at Dean and constantly challenging him. I thought you had lost your damn mind."

She looked at me pointedly. "Guess somebody's got a crush on my fake boyfriend."

She started chuckling again, which had me snickering right along with her.

After I finally caught my breath and Cassie had definitively gotten herself under control, I said, "He encouraged me to come out to you."

Her eyes revealed her affection as she thumped my shoulder. "I'm so glad."

"Why did you feel you had to lie to us about Dean?" I asked after she was quiet for a few seconds.

"I've felt distant from you guys since I've been away and got accustomed to a different way of life," she said. "In retrospect, it was silly. But I didn't want Daddy pushing me about Jerry again."

"I told Daddy to stop insisting that you give him a second chance," I said and her gaze softened. "Cassie, I think Mr. Lorrigan knows I'm gay and that's why he's been spoon feeding the idea to Daddy."

Her eyebrows shot up. "What do you mean?"

"He saw me in town once...with somebody." I swallowed, letting her hear only the one side of it for now. "And I figure he'd never agree to combine our land if he thinks it'd fall to me, the queer son. He wants to entrust it to you and Jerry. Maybe even Braden, but his son would be the better choice from his perspective."

She balled her fists in frustration. "That's just archaic."

I shrugged. "That's reality."

Her fingers brushed my arm. "I'm so sorry."

"It's fine," I said. "I just want us to be close again. And I'm afraid that we have a brother to see through puberty, who might also be..."

Her hand fell away. "Billie? How do you...did you...?"

"Dean told me he suspected it," I said. "I'm fixing to have a talk with Billie. I think it's time anyway. We can't keep treating him like he's going to fall apart at the seams. If we don't step up, he'll get his information from someplace else."

"I agree," she said. "I'll be here for a couple more weeks, so I'd like to help you with that. Lord knows Daddy won't be having that conversation with him."

"Right?" I said. "If Mom were alive, she'd know what to do."

Cassie's smile was tinged with sadness. "She sure would. She'd also give Braden a good talking to. Tell him to call it quits with Jennifer already."

We rode silently for a while, listening to the country station on the radio, each lost in our own thoughts.

"I'm not sure if or when I'll be ready to tell the rest of our family," I said, needing to get it out. "I just..."

"It's okay," she said, turning in her seat. "I understand. Baby steps."

"I'm afraid," I admitted. "About how the business would be affected."

She nodded. "It's sad we live in a world where who you sleep with would matter to a bunch of hunters renting our property."

"They might think I'd tarnished the quail," I said, out of the side of my mouth. "Turned them queer."

Cassie snort laughed and it felt good to be with her again, like old times.

After another minute she asked, "How does Dean fit into all of this?"

"Well, he's your friend and everybody seems to like him," I said. "Billie has sure taken a shine to him."

She smiled tentatively. "Have you?"

I sighed long and hard. Might as well lay it all on the table. "Yeah."

"Is it mutual?" she asked in a soft and soothing voice.

"Pretty sure," I said. "But does it really matter? He'll be on the road soon enough back to that other life you speak so fondly of."

She dropped her head and sat silently thinking the rest of the ride home.

As I drove down the Shady Pines driveway, she said, "Thank you, Callum. I love you."

When I parked, she pulled me into a hug. "I love you, too."

25

DEAN

My knee was jiggling a mile a minute beneath the table.

Grammy informed me that Callum and Cassie had taken some guests in the van to the airport together. I sat eating a muffin and daringly took a bite of some eggs, which were fresh from the coop, and basically amazing.

"Don't worry, he'll be back soon," Grammy said, in the midst of whistling some tune beneath her breath.

When she didn't mention Cassie, only Callum, my gaze flashed to hers. Did she know? But she had already turned away.

After my run, Billie had asked if I'd go riding on the property and I couldn't deny the pull I had to spending time with him again. I needed to ask Cassie about staying longer to attend the festival Billie had told me about. I also wanted to know if Callum had finally told her his news. I was nervous for him, but if I knew Cassie, she would accept that information wholeheartedly.

I was more anxious that she'd be upset about Callum and me. I woke up with the idea that maybe he shouldn't say anything to her at all. But the notion was short-lived because I didn't want to be keeping a secret from Cassie once we both returned to our apartment. I'd prefer to live with the consequences.

When Cassie and Callum hadn't returned by mid-morning, I hopped on the four-wheeler and followed alongside Billie and Bullseye. This time we took a route along the back of the acreage on the other side of the creek. When we came upon a thick fence near an enclosure, Billie slowed down. He motioned for me to pull up closer. "See the gators?"

At first I didn't notice them, until I looked more carefully at eyes and snouts that were resting just above where the water broke the surface. There were several of them swimming in the substantial swamp, their dark bodies blending in with the murky liquid and it made me shiver. They looked so powerful and dangerous. "This is the Lorrigans' land?"

"Yep," he said. "And if we merge someday, this fence will be taken down between our properties."

I watched as beady eyes stared blankly in our direction. "Would it feel strange to have these reptiles as part of your home?"

"Not really," he said, shrugging. "Guess I'm used to them. Grammy's brother used to be an avid gator hunter. She taught me plenty about them. How they run slower on land and have one of the most powerful bites of any reptilian animal. So as long as you respect their true nature, you'll know how to steer clear."

Thinking about how different our upbringing was gave me pause. The fact that this teenager could speak so nonchalantly about living next door to alligators was mind-boggling.

"And this is how people make their money?" I asked. "Hunting gators?"

"People come from all over creation the first week in September," he said. "Though it's legal all year round in our state, you're only allowed so many tags. The Lorrigans breed the alligators in the summer months and then let most of them back into the wild in the fall."

"And that brings in extra revenue for the Montgomerys?" I asked, not sure if a fifteen year old would even know the ins and outs of his family business.

A city kid might not, but Billie definitely knew, because his answer was immediate. "Yeah, between that and shrimping, we can pay the bills around here. Callum talks to Daddy about figuring something else out so that we don't rely on the Lorrigans so much, but it always turns into an argument and nothing gets solved."

I stood gaping at the gators for a long while, just taking in what Billie had confessed. This was Callum's livelihood and that sat heavy in my gut. Not so much that I disapproved of it, now that I understood it better. I only wished that we had met under different circumstances, but any which way I thought about it led to a dead end.

"Can we drive by the sugar canes again?" I asked, wanting a second glance to see if my earlier suspicions had been correct.

We turned the four-wheelers east and began motoring toward the field he had taken me to previously. I climbed off the vehicle and took a better look around. I noticed a small wooden structure near the edge of the tree line next to the iron handle of what resembled an old-fashioned water well. "Is that a shed?"

"Yep, holds garden tools and a hose you can hook up," he said. It resembled a couple others I had seen around the property, in various stages of construction. "But it hasn't been opened since Grammy was out here last year hoping to make some headway."

I strode straight to the door and noticed the rusty hinge. The entryway creaked open and cobwebs hung from the celling. I ignored them and blindly reached for a rake and a hoe. I walked back to the dusty field and Billie watched as I began scraping away some of the dead leaves near one of the rotting canes.

I bent down and began digging in the dirt, turning it up with my fingers and spontaneously making shallow trenches, which would be easier once I watered the area. It would feel so good to get my hands nice and grimy again. I missed my plants at home and here I had an entire field at my disposal.

"What are you doing?" Billie asked in a tickled voice.

"I don't know exactly," I said. "I've got a pretty good green thumb. Let's see what happens."

I remembered that sugar canes were planted horizontally and that they were hardy, only needing to be replaced after several fruitful years. I figured once I aerated the soil, I could use some of the better-looking roots and attempt to replant them.

The sound of a motor rumbled in my ears and I looked up just as Callum was climbing off his vehicle. He repositioned his black ball cap, his copper locks curling enticingly over his ears. When we made eye contact, he smiled, and I let out a breath. "What are you two up to?"

"Billie showed me the gators and then I asked him to bring me back here." Bullseye barked and went off chasing something in the brush. "I wish I had the time to make this field work for you guys."

Callum's mouth dropped open. "You'd want to do that, city boy?"

"For sure, you should see our apartment back home. Cassie says my plants are out of control," I said and I saw a cross between amusement and longing in his eyes. "It would feel awesome to get my hands dirty and see if I can't save some of these plants."

"Think the field can be salvaged?" he asked, watching as my fingers dug grooves into the dirt.

"Won't know unless you try," I said, wiping my forearm across my brow. "I think I was right about the grasshoppers and I'll read up on how to keep them away. But for now I'll replant some of these and maybe we can get some fresh sugar canes in town?"

"We can do that, right Callum?" Billie asked, excitement in his eyes.

"Sure. Probably sell them at Dermot's stand," Callum said. "But I thought you were hitting the road after—"

"I asked Dean to stay for the festival," Billie said, his hands flailing.

I stood up and wiped at my knees. "If that's okay with you, I'd like to stay."

Callum nodded but looked pensive. "Billie, Grammy wants you up at the house. Head back with Bullseye, we'll be right behind you."

"Okay," he said, his eyebrows scrunched together.

"But later you and I are going to talk," Callum said, placing his hand on his shoulder.

"About what?" Billie asked, clapping for his dog to return from the woods.

"Just about some things. You aren't in trouble," he said, sounding like a parent again and it made me grin. "It's something Mom would've done a long time ago."

Billie bit his lip. "Is it the talk that Leo said his parents had with him?"

"He told you that?" Callum asked, his eyebrows shooting to his hairline.

Billie's cheeks colored. "Yeah."

"Well, it's time," Callum said. "Daddy should've done it a while ago. He's been too busy."

But I also got what Callum wasn't saying. His father had probably underestimated that Billie would grow into a typical teenager despite his disabilities.

After Billie took off down the path with Bullseye on his tail, Callum and I stood silently staring at each other. He adjusted his cap on his head and bit at his lip, which told me he was anxious.

"You told Cassie, didn't you?" I asked.

"Yeah," he said, looking down and toeing the dirt.

"And?" My heart was beating out of my chest.

"And I wish we weren't out in the open like this," he said, looking over his shoulder. "So I could kiss you."

I looked behind him toward where the gators had been swimming. All my thoughts that had been swirling about Callum and me being too dissimilar and too far apart, had seemed to fly out the window when he was right in front of me. I stepped closer.

"We're pretty secluded," I said, reaching my fingers out to his. "How did Cassie take it?"

"She was surprised at first," he said, interlacing our hands. "But then she said it made a lot of sense."

"I'll bet," I said, thinking about what Cassie had shared with me about Callum.

"So you don't have to pretend anymore with her," I said and he nodded. "What about the rest of your family?"

"I'm not sure right now," he said, tugging me nearer. Something ticked in his jaw. "I'm just glad I don't have to see the two of you play-acting anymore. I don't want you to..."

A smirk crept across my lips. "You have a possessive streak don't you?"

"I don't know," he said, grabbing me around the waist and hauling me to his chest. "I haven't ever felt this..."

"What do you feel?" I murmured into his neck. "Because I'm wondering how I met a perfect guy who lives such a different life than me."

"I'm not perfect," he said into my hair. "I'm grouchy and proud."

"You definitely are those things." I chuckled. "But I'm not perfect either. I like to argue with you and make you grouchier."

His smile lit up his whole face. "Damn. I just wish we had the chance to date, to see where this might lead."

He rubbed his lips across mine. "I mean, if you'd want to date me."

"I want that as badly as you," I said, sliding my mouth against his again. When his tongue darted out and tangled with mine, I groaned. "But I need to leave after that festival. I have work and my final class this summer."

"And then what?" he asked, something like hope mixed with trepidation in his eyes.

"I don't know," I said, feeling a stinging moment of regret. "It's likely I'll get an offer to work full time in my lab."

He nodded and then yanked me even closer, devouring my mouth in a kiss that made my toes curl.

I dragged my lips away, panting. "What did Cassie say about you and me? Did you tell her?"

"She guessed," he said. "And she didn't have much to say. Only looked bummed."

Apparently Cassie understood the circumstances as well as we did.

We stayed lip-locked for a while longer, our hands in each other's hair, and his ball cap relegated to the ground.

"Only two more days with you," he mumbled against my mouth.

"We couldn't have hidden from your family much longer anyway," I said, kissing his ear. "What would they think if I was hanging with you instead of Cassie?"

"Yeah, I know." The situation seemed so hopeless and he looked so beautiful standing there that my heart lurched in my chest. He bent down and picked up his hat, dusting it off on his knee.

"If we had more time together, I'm afraid I'd only want you more," he said, his voice ragged, his eyes focused somewhere in the distance. "So maybe it's for the best."

"Guess so," I said in a whisper. My stomach dropped as he took a step backward. I wanted desperately to tug him closer to me and hold him for longer.

"Okay if I work on this soil for awhile?" I said, pointing behind me. "I'll meet you back at the house soon."

He smiled. "Dad and Grammy would love that."

26

CALLUM

T hings calmed down on our property after all the guests had finally left. We tried to get back to our routine but with the mess to clean up and Dean still in town, it was anything but. I felt on edge but my skin was also buzzing in anticipation of spending time with him again.

Dean and Cassie played dominoes at the kitchen table with Grammy and Braden, until well past midnight while Billie and I finished building Yankee Stadium on our Xbox game. I fell asleep on the couch and woke up in the middle of the night with an afghan thrown on top of me.

The following morning, Dean and I went for a run and spent some time at Pines Ledge kissing and touching and talking, desperate not to lose any more valuable minutes it seemed. Dean was eager to work in the sugar cane field for a couple hours after that.

After I returned the party chairs to the supplier, I rode out with my father to see Dean's progress. He'd been curious to hear that Dean had planted the new chutes that Cassie had bought at Dermot's roadside stand, as well as impressed that Dean wanted to help at all. I'd admit, seeing him working on his hands and knees in the soil was damn sexy.

After Dean got back to the house, completely sweaty and dirty, I couldn't resist following him down the hall into his room and shutting the door behind me.

"What are you doing?" he ground out. "I'm all—"

"Goddamn hot seeing you like this," I murmured and then shoved him up against the door.

He groaned into the kiss as he gripped my ass and pulled me toward him. Our lips fused together and I buried my tongue deep inside his mouth.

I ripped off his shirt and pinned his hands above his head. He was musky and filthy and it cranked me way the hell up. I dragged my mouth over his salty neck and collarbone, and then buried my nose in his pit. I took a good long sniff, after biting the muscle flexing between his pec and arm.

"Callum," he moaned. "You make me so hard all the damn time. I can barely see straight."

"I wish I could have a whole night with you," I said, sighing into his neck, smelling the soil and dampness in the hollow of his throat. "But then I'd feel your skin on me for months. Pure torture."

"Maybe if we—"

Just then Grammy called for me. "Callum."

"Fuck." I backed away from Dean. "I'm being too careless."

I straightened my shirt and walked out of the room, pretending I needed to get something from the hall closet. "Hold on Grammy, Dean asked where the fresh linens were."

She stood stock still at the end of the hallway, watching me. I pulled out a clean white towel, gave Dean's door a knock, and handed the cloth to him. He grabbed it, not making eye contact, his cheeks flushed. "Thanks," he mumbled.

My gaze met Grammy's across the distance. Her cheeks quirked up in a strange grin and I thrust the idea from my head that she knew about Dean and me. I couldn't go there right then. I was taking thoughtless risks, but he'd be gone in a couple of day's time and I'd only have my memories, which was better than anything I had before.

"What did you need, Grammy?" I mumbled.

"Help bringing out those large crates for our booth," she said, motioning behind her to the pantry.

"Selling your fig preserves tomorrow?" I asked, heading her way. That's when I noticed my father sitting at the table drinking a large glass of sweet tea, rolling his neck side to side. He looked beat so I knew this week had been hard on him.

"That's right," she said, patting my father on the shoulder. "Billie helped me make some strawberry rhubarb pies as well."

I loved that Billie baked with Grammy, and was pretty certain that was why they had seemed so chummy lately. She probably knew more of his secrets these days than I did.

The rest of the afternoon was spent prepping for the county fair. Daddy agreed to rest for a spell while Dean drove into town with Cassie and me as we picked up supplies. We also stopped by my aunt's furniture shop to visit and browse. She begged me for more pieces and I promised to work on additional chairs that summer.

Dean and I were only able to sneak in alone time here or there, with lingering kisses in the hallway or at the sugar cane field. He completed his garden project using chicken manure that Braden had assisted in supplying him and entrusted me to help the field come to fruition in the coming months. We avoided the subject of planning a return visit, both afraid to make any promises that we couldn't keep. But at least our link was Cassie and I could ask about him from time to time.

Early the following morning, our cars loaded, we headed to the fair. Shady Pines Preserve ran a booth offering a sneak peek into our business. We handed out fliers, discount coupons, and had a drawing at the end of the day that included a free pass to the shooting range. We offered some hunting supplies, and Grammy's baked goods always sold like hotcakes.

Bullseye wore his distinct red harness today to alert the public that he was a specially trained medical dog. But most people in this town recognized him, calling Bullseye by name but steering clear of petting him since he was officially *working*.

"Maybe this time next year we'll be selling Montgomery's Sweet syrup," Billie said, patting Bullseye as he beamed at Dean.

"Wouldn't that be something?" Grammy said. "My grand-daddy would be proud."

Dean blushed but I could tell he felt grateful for the shout out as well as a bit pleased.

After Billie met up with Leo, he begged Daddy to take off for a couple of hours to play some carnival games. Dean looked at me knowingly as Daddy handed him a wad of singles. Normally the booth was left to Grammy and me anyway, since this was the business end for me.

Braden got bored with it all too easily, and he and Daddy moved along to socialize with the townsfolk. When Jennifer came calling for my brother, I pointed in the direction of the sheep shearing pen, which Daddy seemed to have his eye on earlier. We'd discussed keeping some ewes on our property in the past as a possible source of extra income, so maybe seeing them had sparked his interest again.

Cassie took Dean around to the other stands, attempting to avoid Jerry, who was working the Lorrigans' booth in the next aisle over. Dean tasted boiled peanuts, a funnel cake, which he declared delicious, and turned his nose at the Hot Beef Sundae, a county fair favorite from the Cattle Association. They apparently ended up at the pig races and he got to see firsthand how our small town operated. It might send him screaming back to the city early for all I knew.

Dean hung around our booth for a while that afternoon, asking Grammy if she got her figs from the tree he'd noticed in the orchard and then moseyed across the way to the university booth that distributed pamphlets about classes.

The next time I looked up he was speaking animatedly to my old professor in the agricultural department. I had a sneaking suspicion that he was asking about sugar cane yields and herbicides. Right in that instant, I could actually picture Dean living here, in this setting. I knew that was just my mind playing tricks on me. Wishful thinking. So I forced the thought aside.

Cassie had wandered off to Dermot's fruit stand. She attempted to appear unassuming since she was supposed to be here with Dean and my stomach tightened around the idea that we were all pretending in one way or another.

She'd be free to pursue whomever she pleased as soon as Dean left. That thought sat like a lead balloon in my gut. She could've told Daddy the truth, at least for Dermot's sake, but what did it matter if Dean would be gone this time tomorrow?

As dusk fell, we wrapped up our booth, and found spots on the hillside to watch the fireworks display that always concluded this day. Dean sat beside Cassie and I was on his other side, our shoulders brushing every now and again, sending chills up my spine.

Braden had met up with Jennifer, and Grammy and Daddy sat in front of us, making small talk with Dermot and his family. Daddy looked more relaxed and animated than yesterday and I knew that all he needed was a breather from the pressure of it all. Eventually Dermot moved to sit beside Cassie, fuck what the town might think.

Billie and Leo were sitting behind us whispering and snickering and I could feel Bullseye's soft fur on my leg. That's when I spotted Jason with his new boyfriend, Brian, across the way. Something seared hot in my chest. It wasn't envy, more like a profound sadness that I'd never have what Jason did. I'd never be that open.

Once the fireworks began, everyone's attention was diverted to the sky, and I could observe Jason more openly. He sat proudly next to his new guy, who was good-looking with his strong jaw and shaggy brown hair. They weren't holding hands, so nothing was obvious on the surface, but their knees were touching and they were smiling and laughing. I could tell they were a couple, could anybody else?

"This is amazing," Dean said in a low voice next to me.

I smiled, tearing my eyes away from Jason. "They put on a great display."

"You seem distracted," Dean said, his thigh grazing mine and I shivered. "Someone you know?"

"It's Jason and his new boyfriend," I said low enough for only his ears.

A flicker of something unreadable crossed over his features. "Jealous?"

"No, not in the way you'd think," I said. "More so it's...envy over what he has."

"You can have that too, you know," Dean said. "If you really wanted to. Even if only those closest to you knew the real deal."

I met his gaze as the vivid lights from the pyrotechnics made his eyes appear opalescent. Almost like ice. His emotions were trapped just below the surface—melancholy and hope, caution and affection. I wanted to grab firm hold of him and slam my mouth over his lips. Or at the very least, entangle our fingers together.

"I mean," he continued, his eyes revealing more of his vulnerability. "If you found the right guy to be with."

The low murmur of the crowd lulled me into a false sense of security. "I think I might have found him. Though I'd like more time to assess that theory."

When my pinkie finger swiped against his on the grass, he inhaled deeply, as if I had stroked his face. His eyelids fluttered as his chest heaved from his substantial breaths.

"If only he didn't live in a different state," I mumbled.

Something like a low moan released from his throat. It sounded carnal and needy and I wished I could lay him down in the grass and mash my lips against his, taste his tongue, feel its weight in my mouth.

We sat with our fingers touching for a few stolen moments. It felt like a tender caress as my skin buzzed with an awareness of him being so close yet entirely too far away.

"You'd get sick of me soon enough anyway," he said. "My eating habits. My liberal views on hunting and guns. Though you've definitely opened my eyes to several things."

"Don't assume I'm some conservative NRA card holder. I would support more regulations. Too much gun violence in this country," I said, reining in my exasperation. I hated that he would dismiss the idea of an *us* so easily. "We have yet to discuss the real hot button issues of politics and religion."

"True," he said. "I'm sure we'd get into a fight or two. Or ten. But making up sure would be fun."

The pounding and popping of the grand finale drowned out any further conversation and we looked up at the sky in awe until it was all over and the crowd was on their feet heading toward the exit.

Jason made his way over to us with his boyfriend as we gathered up our blankets. Introductions were made and Jason looked at me perceptively, figuring Dean was the guy I had talked about on the phone.

"Hey, we're heading up to The Stampede," Jason said. It was a dive bar that was a ways out of town, off the main freeway. A place few people would recognize us. "Want to meet up?"

Dean looked over at Cassie, who stood next to Dermot. "You guys go ahead. I, uh..."

She motioned behind her trying to come up with some crazy excuse to have Dermot drive her home, no doubt. Suddenly Grammy butted into the conversation. "You young'uns go on ahead. I'll let your daddy know you're off doing something fun. We'll take Billie home."

She smiled at Cassie and me and then caught up with my dad.

When we got to the parking lot, Cassie blushed and mumbled in my ear, "We might meet you at the bar. If not, see you at home."

Dean and I followed Jason and Brian to The Stampede and sat in a shabby vinyl booth in the back of the bar to have some beers. It felt so damn good to be there with Dean and to talk openly with people who understood me.

I'd admit it was awkward having my old lover meet my current one.

But truth be told, nothing held a candle to Dean. Nothing.

"So you're out and proud where you live?" Jason asked Dean, sipping at his beer.

"Yeah," Dean said. "It's more accepted. Few people bat an eyelash. How about you guys?"

"It's not so bad around the larger cities like Gainesville and Jacksonville," he said and I could feel Dean's gaze searing into the side of my face. But my family's business wasn't in the big city. It was in the rural town of Roscoe more than an hour away from any city.

Dean spoke more about his work in the lab and Jason talked about his job and future travel plans. With every passing minute, I was itching to get the hell out of there so I could spend my last moments with Dean alone, even if it was in a car ride back to the preserve.

"Well, it was great meeting you, Dean," Jason said, as we headed toward the exit. "Hope to see you again sometime."

27

DEAN

As we got in the truck, the mood was solemn. Like there was a finality to this, our last night together. My time here was coming to a close.

"Do you want to..." Callum's voice was hoarse, as if he couldn't get enough air.

"What?" I rasped, my voice cracking as well.

Callum swallowed and his eyes looked weary and sad. "Will you go someplace with me? Someplace private? I just need—"

"Yes," I said, my answer instantaneous. "I need it, too."

My fingers reached out to rest on his knee because I couldn't help touching him. His lids lowered and he inhaled through his nose as his hand covered mine.

He drove for a while on the main roads before finally making a few left turns and pulling down a remote looking dirt road. It became darker the further we progressed and eventually he swerved off the embankment past some tall cypress trees and slowed near a small pond.

Once he dimmed the headlights, the solo source of illumination came from the blanket of twinkling stars surrounding a full moon. Small splashes and the croak of bullfrogs added a quaint backdrop to the serenity of the night.

It was pretty—magical, really. And there didn't seem to be a soul around for miles. It was as if we had discovered our own private nook.

"I haven't been back here since high school," Callum said. As soon as he cut the engine, I didn't know who moved first.

Our mouths and bodies met. Hands burrowing in hair, lips sucking on necks and ears and jaws. Our tongues were sliding and battling and I couldn't taste him fast enough or anywhere near my fill.

Callum broke away panting hard.

"Wait," he said, shifting his leg over the seat. He leaned over to search through his glove box for something, coming up empty handed, while I gave him a peck on the ear. "It's too tight of a fit in here. Let's get out of the truck."

"Outside?" I said, staring through the windshield at the dark night. "Are there any gators out there?"

"Don't worry, I'll defend you," he said, grinning.

He reached for a couple of blankets from his back seat and yanked on my hand to exit the truck.

"Not funny," I mumbled, searching the ground below me as I got my footing.

He pulled down the tailgate at the rear of the truck and tossed the blankets on the flatbed.

As soon as he smoothed out the soft corners and sat down in the middle of the spread, he reached for me. "Come here."

I placed my knee on the end of the bumper to haul myself up and then straddled his legs.

His hands curled beneath the back of my shirt and met skin as he tugged me flush against him. Our lips and groins slid together and I moaned, loving the idea of finally feeling him without the worry of anybody walking in on us.

We kissed in that position for slow lingering minutes, our lips resting together while our tongues explored in a gentle and languid pace. Finally he lifted my thighs and nudged me aside.

He yanked off his shirt and shoved his jeans down while I did the same. He towed me over to kneel between his legs as my hard cock tented the material of my underwear. His palms slid beneath the back of my briefs to squeeze my bare ass.

When his mouth teased my length through the front panel, I cried out.

"Fuck, Callum," I panted, my fingernails biting into his shoulders. "Feels so good."

He made a noise in the back of his throat before yanking down my briefs and sucking the head of my cock into the hot furnace of his mouth. I whimpered as his tongue licked around the crown and then into the slit to collect the pre-come gathered there.

Callum hummed as his mouth engulfed my entire length. My eyes practically rolled into the back of my head as my hands dug into his scalp.

His fingers found my crease and he teased my crack, swirling around the hole, which contracted at his touch. "You like that?"

"Mmmmm," I murmured, already so close to losing my load. "Do you have any lube?"

"I don't have anything with me," he said and now I understood why he was rummaging around his car before we got out. "Was hoping you did."

My eyes darted to his as disappointment made my shoulders slump. "I don't. I never expected on this trip to—"

"It doesn't matter," he said cutting me off. "I just want my mouth all over you. I hate the taste of lube anyway."

My knees began trembling at his words. He kissed my belly and then took a deep sniff of the patch of hair at my groin.

"I want to eat your ass and make you open up for my fingers." His tongue licked along my length as his hands gripped my cheeks. "Would you like that?"

"Please," I whispered. "But I want to taste you too."

He sat up suddenly and pushed down his briefs, his gorgeous cock jutting out, flushed and leaking. I wanted to get my lips around it as soon as possible. He lay down on the blanket facing sideways and encouraged me to lie the opposite way.

Without any further words spoken we began sucking each other off. He was so thick that I had a hard time getting my mouth around him. But if his moans were any indication, he seemed to like it when I ran my tongue up and down the underside of his cock and then suctioned the head.

Breathing through my nose, I took him further by relaxing my throat. But it was so hard to concentrate because he was performing magic tricks with his tongue. He had my balls in his mouth as he nibbled and sucked me into submission. I was squirming against him, the hairs on my legs prickling.

I dropped lower, licking around his sac, pulling his balls between my lips, and releasing them with a pop. I loved discovering the patches of red hair everywhere even around his smooth pink hole as my fingers explored the crease of his ass. I stretched my head to rest my chin behind his balls so that I could spread his cheeks apart with my thumbs.

I rubbed my tongue around his perineum and then licked a stripe across his asshole. He stilled as a groan emitted from deep in his chest. He smelled like Callum—musk and earth and pine and I couldn't get enough as my tongue circled and jabbed at his hole.

I could feel his cock resting against my neck and leaking down my chest.

"Come here, you," he said in a hoarse voice. He shifted his torso, grabbed hold of my hips, and hauled my body on top of his, my ass in his face. Fuck.

He parted my cheeks and the first slash of his tongue made me gasp. He licked and speared at my hole. I was open mouth panting into his groin, sucking the head of his cock every now and again but unable to get a handle on my breathing, it felt so electric.

It was as if all the nerve endings in my body had converged in one area, making me drunk with overwhelming pleasure.

Callum moved again, grabbing hold of my thighs in his callused palms and lifting me up. "I want to tongue fuck you."

"Goddamn, Callum," I said, gripping his waist for leverage. "I'm close to losing my mind."

My cheeks were split open and I could feel his thumbs digging into my hole and spreading me even wider. "Sit on my tongue."

"Shit. Goddamn." My legs began quivering as my fingers braced my thighs and I lowered myself to his mouth. As his tongue pushed its way inside me, my ass clenched and I stilled, a bolt of lightning shooting straight to my cock.

I lost all sense of time and place, my vision going white hot as intense bliss seized my body and locked my limbs.

"Holy fuck." I came with a shout, ribbons of seed surging against my stomach. There was so much come that it dripped down to his chest and dampened the patch of hair between his pecs.

Callum groaned when he felt my spunk trickle onto his skin. "So damn hot," he muttered, kissing my hole and then licking and biting my cheeks.

It was the most intimate I'd ever been with anybody, and that was certainly one of the most powerful orgasms I'd ever experienced. I couldn't talk or move, my heartbeat still thundering in my ears, as he continued to feather his lips over my backside.

This country boy had rendered me speechless.

28

DEAN

I finally rolled off of Callum, and curled on my side, my legs still trembling.

He chuckled. "Are you dead?"

"If I am, then I'm flying high in the clouds somewhere," I mumbled into the blanket. "That was incredible. I just need a moment."

I opened my lids and stared at him—his eyes crinkled with a smile, his lips swollen, and his face flushed. He was stunning.

He lifted onto his knees and began pumping his very stiff cock. "Damn, that's a sight."

Warm puffs of air wafted over my skin, making me shiver. "It won't take me long after seeing you come apart like that."

I flattened myself on the blanket and grabbed hold of his thigh. "I want you to come on my chest."

He straddled my waist and angled his hips toward me with a groan. I sucked on my fingers and reached beneath his sac. His hole was still softened from my tongue so I worked a digit inside him fairly easily.

"Fuck," he grunted, snapping his thighs and riding my hand as I niggled a second finger inside.

"Is that good?" I asked, watching him shamelessly propel his hips in a seductive dance.

"So good," he said, biting his lip. "I love having fingers up my asshole. Maybe as much as you liked having my tongue."

Pumping in and out of him, I wished we had days, weeks, months to explore all the ways to work over each other's bodies like this.

I watched in wonder as a crimson flush spread up his torso, across his shoulders, reaching his neck and cheeks. His luminescent skin nearly matched the color of his hair.

His back arched, his mouth fell open, and he came with a growl all over my chest, some even spurting across my jaw. I kept my fingers buried inside his body and felt his muscles constrict around them, wishing it could be my cock instead.

Except maybe if it was my cock, I'd feel even more wrecked about leaving him. Suddenly my final class and my job at the lab seemed insubstantial, even knowing they were necessary to graduate early.

Eventually Callum opened his eyes and looked down at the mess he'd made as I pulled my fingers from inside him. He shivered as a strange expression crossed his face. He bent over me and his tongue gently outlined my lips as he stared into my eyes.

I was entranced as his fingers began pressing into my skin, as if infusing his come, much like that night at the oak tree.

He sank on top of me and his lips slipped lazily against mine. We lay still and silent, neither willing to let the other go as palms traced over skin and nails tunneled through hair.

"What were you doing?" I whispered. "Rubbing your come into my chest?"

"I just...I want you to remember me." His eyes darted away, as if he'd been caught doing something deviant. "Magical thinking, I guess. I know it's stupid."

"It's not stupid," I said, trying unsuccessfully to capture his gaze. "I thought it was beautiful. I think *you're* beautiful."

"I think you are too," he mumbled as he nuzzled my shoulder.

I cupped his chin forcing him to meet my eyes. "Besides, how could I ever forget one of the best nights of my life?"

His gaze softened and it seemed he was going to say something deep but instead he dragged me into such an intense and overwhelming kiss that I thought my heart might explode.

We kissed listlessly for a long while, almost drifting off to sleep, as our lips stayed connected, breathing the same air.

Callum finally shifted to untangle our legs. "We need to head back."

We dressed mechanically, neither making much eye contact, as a heaviness cloaked the silence between us. We got buckled in the truck and held hands the entire way home.

He only let my fingers go when he pulled onto Shady Pines property and I felt the warm air shift away from me.

The house was dark as we walked inside and Callum kissed my temple as he shut the door behind us. As soon as we reached the kitchen we heard it. Bullseye whining and scratching at something. Callum's eyes widened and he darted down the hall, throwing open Billie's door.

When I reached his room and searched over Callum's shoulder, Billie was thrashing in his bed, his arms flexing, his back bowing stiffly, his eyes rolling in the back of his head. Bullseye stayed along the edge closest to the floor possibly in an effort to protect him from pitching forward and hitting his head.

"Billie, you're having a seizure," Callum said, loud enough for the house to hear as he stepped inside the room. "It's okay, I'm here. You'll get through it."

By the time the seizure was over, the entire household was awake, standing inside his room. I had moved aside to allow his family to get by. Feeling like an intruder at that moment, I made myself as small as possible in the far corner by the closet door.

"He hasn't had one in months," Cassie whispered to me as

Billie's body gradually stopped convulsing and Callum swept his sweaty hair out of his eyes.

"What brings them on?" I asked, trying to remain quiet and obscure.

"Hard to say," she said, twisting her lip. "Sometimes stress, sleep deprivation, hormones. His body chemistry is off." At his age, Billie was smack dab in the middle of puberty. That period of time feels crazy in any teen's life let alone suffering through it alongside a seizure disorder.

As Billie blinked open his eyes he looked around the space in a dreamlike state. Bullseye was licking his face and whining a little but not as loudly as before.

"Hey ,kiddo. Bullseye warned you about a seizure," Callum said. "You were probably sleeping heavy and he had a hard time waking you before it began."

"I'm sorry, buddy," Billie said, slurring his words as he reached for his dog.

"In the past, Bullseye has been able to rouse him before the seizure begins so he can get to a safer location on the floor," Cassie said.

That explained why the dog was teetering on the edge of the bed at the opposite side of the wall. "That's incredible."

Grammy stretched down and kissed Billie on the head. "If another happens this week, we'll make a doctor's appointment in town. But you, young man, are going to start getting to bed on time."

I couldn't help feeling guilty for the nights I had contributed to his sleep deficiency with the Xbox. No wonder Callum was so strict that one time.

"For sure," Callum said and suddenly I felt invisible and my leaving inconsequential. Billie's seizure disorder was a way more important thing to worry about than me driving off in a few hours. Callum had his family to take care of. I could understand why he stayed close by.

Billie's gaze darted around the room and landed on me. "You're leaving in the morning."

I gave him an imperceptive nod, not wanting to draw attention to myself. Callum stared at the wall, I noticed, instead of turning his gaze to me.

"Callum..." Billie garbled and hunkered down in his sheets, his eyes drooping. I'd heard that you could sleep for hours after a seizure, that it takes a lot out of you. "Callum's going to miss you."

"I think you mean Cassie," Mr. Montgomery suddenly spoke up, as he cleared his throat.

"No, I mean Callum," Billie said, in a lethargic voice. "He needs somebody like Dean."

Billie closed his eyes and seemed to have fallen asleep instantaneously. Braden yawned and headed toward the door. "He's just confused. Let him get his rest."

He left the room on the heels of his father and the only family remaining in the room were Grammy, Cassie, Callum, and I. The air was thick with tension.

But then Grammy headed toward the hallway. "I reckon so," she mumbled under her breath.

"I'm going to stay for another minute to be sure he's sleeping soundly," Callum said in a level voice, but his eyes were filled with emotion.

Callum and I stared at each other across the room until Cassie cleared her throat. "I'm going to bed."

"Me too," I said, following behind, but Callum caught hold of my hand before I was able to get out the door.

He didn't look at me, just tangled our fingers together and applied pressure. I could feel his pulse pounding through his skin. I think it was his way of saying goodbye and a sob nearly tore from my throat.

I wanted to stay. I needed to go. I wished that somehow we could be together. It was an impossible situation. And as my heart battered in my ears, it felt like it might stop beating all together.

When he finally let go of my hand, I practically bolted through the door overcome with too much heartache.

I tossed and turned for the next couple of hours before getting up and quietly packing the rest of my bag.

I sent Cassie a goodbye text that she'd read in the morning, since I knew she turned off her phone at night.

Then I scrawled Callum a note from a pad I found in the bedside table and carefully slipped it beneath his bedroom door.

Callum,

I didn't want a messy goodbye. It was hard enough to leave you.

But I wanted to thank you. This was probably one of the best trips of my life and it was mostly due to meeting you.

You're grouchy as hell but you make up for it with that sweet mouth.

And you're still one of the smartest and most decent men I've ever met.

Please give Billie my number. You can use it too if you want to stay in touch.

I'd like that very much.

Yours,

Dean

As I pulled out of the driveway, my thumb swiped away the single tear that had escaped my eye.

29

CALLUM

My chest burned so hot. Like there was a hole where my heart had been. Dean had stolen away at dusk a couple of days ago and left me a note that I'd probably read a dozen times by now.

It was quiet around the house, everybody concerned about Billie and whether his seizures would be triggered again. But he had slept in and looked well rested that afternoon and evening.

He admitted he'd been getting less sleep and I had a sneaking suspicion that he was busy texting Leo. Not that I was blaming the kid, Billie was as much at fault as he was. When you're young, you do sneaky things, and talking in the middle of the night was the least of any sins.

I was glad that everyone's focus was elsewhere because that gave me time to try to regroup. It felt different here without Dean, and that was ridiculous because his visit had been short, relatively speaking, so I needed to pull my head out of my ass.

Cassie and Grammy seemed to be walking on eggshells around me because I was back to my grumpy old self, maybe even worse. I could tell Cassie wanted to say something reassuring but I cut her off at the pass with a stern look. Grammy, on the other hand, just kept plying me with food and asked Billie to whip up a batch of my favorite brownies.

Dad and Braden remained clueless, so guess I really was this moody all the time.

I received a text from Dean late last night and it made me wonder if he was having as much trouble sleeping as I was.

Dean: Just letting you know I'm home safe. And that you're on my mind.

Me: Thanks for letting me know. And ditto.

Dean: I wish it could be different.

Me: Me too.

Dean: Hope Billie is okay?

Me: He will be.

Truth be told, I was done hiding around my family. I figured I couldn't feel any shittier, so why not just put it all on the table. Maybe Dean was right. Maybe only the important people in my life needed to know and I could deal with the rest as it came.

But the idea of disappointing my father made my chest constrict so tight, I could scarcely catch my breath. First, I needed to get on the same page with another member of my family.

I took a slow ride out to the sugar cane field with Billie on the back of my four-wheeler. He kept huffing disapprovingly over my shoulder because I wouldn't increase my speed after the scare we had. He wouldn't be able to drive himself for a while, nor apply for a regular state license any time soon, until we had the situation under control. It was more important to keep him safe, but I definitely felt for him.

Cutting the engine, we hopped off the vehicle to have a look around. After all of the work Dean had put in, I wanted to make sure we kept up with the progress. Maybe we could actually make something of this plot of land. I smiled at his neat rows of plants and the small marker that indicated new cuttings.

Billie stood beside me as I stuck my toe in the dirt. "You miss him, don't you?"

"Yes," I said without hesitation. It felt good to voice it out loud. "But I'll survive."

"If he lived closer," he said in a cautious voice. "Would you try to date him?"

My eyebrow quirked. Guess we were finally going there.

"Definitely," I said, meeting his eyes. "Got something to tell me, little brother?"

"I...I guess..." he sputtered. "Leo's my best friend but it's turned into something more."

My stomach knotted for my brother. "Does he feel the same way?"

"I think so," he said, turning away, and searching for a stick to throw for Bullseye.

I found a decent one laying in the grass so I picked it up and handed it to him. "Has anything happened between the two of you?"

A flush arose on his cheeks. "He kissed me the night of the fireworks."

God, so innocent. I wished I'd had somebody to share all that with when I was his age. Though he'd figured it out way sooner.

"I had trouble sleeping that night," he said in a tentative voice, as if I'd scold him. "It felt so good and I want him to do it again."

"Oh, buddy. I get it," I said, squeezing his shoulder. "But you have a medical condition and you want to be around to experience all of it with him or whoever you give your heart to, right? Which means getting more sleep."

"Leo feels terrible about what happened," Billie said. "He's upset he had something to do with it..."

Poor kid. I made a mental note to have a talk with him next time he was over. Maybe lay down some ground rules.

"He's not afraid to get to know me," Billie said, stroking Bullseye's neck. "The other kids at school, they keep their distance, you know?"

My heart felt so heavy in my chest as we stood side by side staring at the horizon.

"You know what, little brother?" I said, looping my arm around his neck. "You might end up being way braver than me."

He shrugged. "What will Daddy say?"

"I'm not sure," I said. "But it's time for me to make the path easier for you to navigate."

After I dropped off Billie near the porch, I drove the four-wheeler into the garage, and parked next to the other two. They'd need tune-ups soon enough. We usually left that in Braden's hands. He was the most mechanically inclined out of all of us.

When I heard some raised voices out by the chicken coop, I crept around the corner to listen. It was my dad and Mr. Lorrigan. He must've stopped by to pick up the extra chairs they'd let us borrow for the reception.

"Cassie all but ignored Jerry," Mr. Lorrigan was saying.

"I reckon you're just making excuses now. My daughter brought home a nice young man," Dad said and I cringed. "Nothing I can do to change that. You either want to merge or you don't. Put up or shut up. Either way, I'm too tired to talk about it."

Daddy stormed off toward the house and after waiting a second longer, I cut Mr. Lorrigan off at the pass. He nearly tripped over his own two feet; I had startled him so badly.

"This will be the last year we help you with overflow, not unless you want to throw us a bigger bone," I said, attempting to keep my hands at my side, lest I throttle him. "For the record, the offer to merge is officially off the table."

"You think I'd let a faggot stake a claim in my business?" he said, his teeth clenched. "I saw you with that young man. Disgusting."

I braced myself, my entire body flushing in shame. But another emotion quickly took center stage. Blinding fury. "So the truth finally comes out."

"That's right," he said, standing ramrod straight. "What do you got to say about it?"

"Plenty. I may be gay but what you are is repulsive," I said, jabbing my finger at him. "Let's not forget that I saw you, too. You're a cheater, going into that woman's room."

His eyes grew wide and his mouth hung open. "You don't know—"

"Why else would you be at a hotel only an hour away from home?" I asked, folding my arms.

"You've got no proof," he stammered. He stared at me vacantly, his mind reeling.

"Proof?" I said. "What is this, the Jerry Springer show? I've got my solid reputation to fall back on."

"Your reputation won't be worth squat when I—"

"If you plan on scattering any rumors to ruin our business, then I've got gossip to spread as well," I said. "I'll let your wife know exactly what I saw. You better hope your family forgives you."

His face turned tomato red and as he balled his fists I was certain he was going to try to hit me.

"I've done nothing wrong except be exactly who I am. But you've broken a sacred vow. You've got to live with yourself. And unfortunately, so does your family," I said, raising my voice. "Now get the hell off my property."

He practically sprinted to his truck and peeled away.

I thought I heard a door slam shut somewhere in the distance but it just as well could've been my brain splintering into a million pieces.

30

CALLUM

The next couple of days we welcomed some hunting groups and I fell back into my regular routine, even though it seemed less satisfying. I attempted to run the trail up to Pines Ledge but it felt empty without Dean. They say it takes twenty-one days to form a habit, but he was here for shorter and I already felt so addicted.

The only time I was able to get out of my own head was when I finally stepped inside the sawmill again with some newly chopped wood. I dusted off the circular saw and took stock of supplies; making a mental note to buy more red paint for the new chairs I had promised my aunt.

"Glad to see you back to doing something you love," Cassie had said when she walked by the small workroom on the way back from changing the linens in the cabin.

I looked forward to Dean's regular texts and tried not to be disappointed if I hadn't heard from him in some time. I didn't know why I kept talking to him even though I knew a relationship was a dead end. But the fact of the matter was that I now also considered him a friend.

He was back to working in his lab and would be starting his

final summer class. He apparently graduated in September but wouldn't officially get his degree until December. Though he could always start looking for a job and if he was asked to stay on in a full-time position at the university, that would be a no-brainer.

Of course Dean inquired about how his sugar cane field was holding up. And in some twisted way, it was a link to him that I needed right then. Since it took a long time for the plant to germinate and mature before it could be harvested, it was important to keep the weeds to a minimum and the grasshoppers from getting to the leaves once they sprouted.

Dean admitted he had been asking my old professor about an effective herbicide at the county fair that one day. Apparently they had exchanged email information, so he was waiting to hear back on the best solution. Grammy was especially excited about the sugar canes and I overheard her talking to Cassie about making it part of our business model to supplement our revenue.

I had yet to tell Daddy about my argument with Mr. Lorrigan, but he seemed too busy to talk to me anyway, already gone in the early morning hours and coming home late. And Cassie's mind was completely absorbed with Dermot. But I didn't blame her because I was having the same problem.

We were finally all together at the dinner table the following night, Grammy making it known that we were to show up and eat as a family. You did not mess with Grammy's orders, so when we heard the supper bell clang, we all dropped whatever it was that we were doing.

"You're seeing Dermot again tonight?" Braden asked Cassie, wiggling his eyebrows. Dermot had picked Cassie up at the house last night and she had come home late.

"Maybe," Cassie said. Her eyes flitted to me briefly before she finally said, "I want to see him as much as I can while I'm in town. What's wrong with that?"

"Nothing as far as I can tell," Braden said, shrugging. "The folks at Sunnyside Up Diner will have something new to talk about at least."

"Let them talk all they want," Grammy said. "You're just happy they'll stop gossiping about how long before you and Jennifer get married and have babies."

Braden groaned, his neck coloring pink, as he took another bite of Grammy's chicken fried steak.

"What am I missing here?" Daddy asked around a mouthful of mashed potatoes as Grammy snickered. "What happened to Dean?"

Cassie cringed and I kicked her leg beneath the table as a well of panic arose in my gut.

She shook her head and braced her jaw. "Dean and I are really just friends. He's my..."

"Friends?" Daddy said. "So why would you—"

"Please let me get this out," she said and Daddy chewed his meal quietly. "I didn't feel like answering anybody's questions about whether Jerry and I would get back together. I just wanted to come home and enjoy my visit."

Daddy's face fell as if he knew he'd screwed up one way or another when it came to his weak arrangement with the Lorrigans.

"Honey, nobody at this table wants you to be with Jerry," Grammy said. "Your daddy knows it's not meant to be. I don't think Mr. Lorrigan's intentions are as pure as you might think."

Grammy shot a look in my direction and it felt like a boulder had lodged in my throat. She never missed a beat.

"Go on, Cassie," Daddy said, his eyebrows scrunched together. "I'd like to hear what else you have to say."

"Dean is actually my roommate and before you go off on a tangent about me living with a guy—which is totally antiquated in today's day and age—just know he is the perfect male friend to have," she said in one rambling sentence. "Not only is he smart and kind and supportive, he's gay, and I have his permission to tell you all, now that we're no longer pretending."

Daddy's fork stopped midway to his mouth and I thought he might drop it and make a splattering mess. Braden looked just as thunderstruck, his eyebrows knitting together. I pushed back from the table, having lost my appetite, along with my resolve.

"Gay?" Braden asked at practically the same time as Daddy said, "Dean is gay?"

Daddy's gaze darted to mine all of a sudden—his eyes flaring —as if putting two and two together.

And then it hit me. The sound of the screen door slapping shut yesterday. "You heard my conversation with Mr. Lorrigan didn't you?"

He nodded, his gaze filling with apology and sadness. "I was going to talk to you about it, son. I'm not very good at...I just needed time..."

"Will somebody please fill me in?" Braden said. "How is Dean gay? He doesn't look like a queer."

"What the hell do you think gay people look like?" I asked, exasperated.

I could see Billie stiffen in my side view. He knew better than to open his mouth during a serious adult discussion at the table, but this indirectly affected him and I knew he had plenty to say.

"Hell, I don't know," Braden said, flicking his wrist. "Maybe like, fruity. Effeminate."

"Way to stereotype, brother," I said, throwing up my hands.

"Well, stereotypes are true for a reason," he shot back at me all smug.

"Then you're truly a dumb redneck," I said and I could hear Grammy snicker into her drink. "And you can pigeonhole me too, because *I'm* gay."

My head became fuzzy and lightheaded and I felt Billie shift beside me as a muffled gasp arose from Braden. I placed my hand on Billie's knee to clam him up. He'd have his say on the subject way later, after all of this blew over.

My gaze finally lifted to meet Braden's across the table. I'd have plenty of battles to fight from here on in, so I didn't want to back down from my own brother. I waited for him to ask me about the girl *Sheila* I always said I was meeting in town, but he only stared at me, his eyes blown wide, as he attempted to wrap his brain around the idea.

"I'm proud of you, Callum," Grammy said and my heart rose to my throat. Tears were threatening to escape but I swallowed them down.

"Me too, son," Daddy said in a pained voice and my eyes sprang to his. "I'm proud of all of my kids. I just don't always have the right words or answers. If your mother were around..." he broke off, still choked up at the thought of my mother gone after all these years.

"She'd tell us we were some eclectic bunch," Grammy said and Cassie smiled. "She'd also say *to hell* with the Lorrigans."

Everybody chuckled in relief except Billie who sat rigid and awkward beside me.

"Billie," Daddy said in a strangled whisper. "She would've protected and cared for you most of all."

Tears burst from Billie's eyes and rolled down his cheeks in fat drops.

His chair clattered on the linoleum floor as he bounded from his seat and threw himself into Daddy's arms. The entire table grew silent as we watched them and even Braden dabbed at his eyes.

A couple minutes later, Grammy stood up to deliver Billie's homemade key lime pie to the center of the table.

"He made it special for you," Grammy said to Daddy. "Your favorite."

Daddy offered his youngest son a watery grin and we all dug in as Billie slid pieces of pie to the dessert plates in front of us.

Chewing gave us a reprieve from all of our heavy emotions. Braden continued to stare at me across the table as if seeing me in a new light.

Once we were nearly finished with our slices, Daddy cleared his throat. "I wish I knew how to make it on our own without the Lorrigans help."

I placed my fork down. "I'm sorry that my being gay might mean that people shy away from our business."

Braden scrunched up his face as if just realizing the full implications. "Screw them."

"Easier said than done. I mean, if we keep this under wraps in our family that's cool. But I don't want to keep pretending forever." Billie grabbed for my hand and I squeezed back. "It doesn't feel good to hide."

"You want to know what I think?" Cassie said, after licking her fork clean.

"Please," Daddy said. "I can see you've been stewing on something."

"I'll be graduating with my master's in business this fall," she said. "I think after I move back home we regroup and start changing tactics."

"How?" Braden said, pushing back in his seat and patting his stomach.

"We take our ancestors' lead," she said, placing our empty plates in a pile. "They changed with the times. Tried different things. We should too."

"What exactly do you mean?" Daddy said, adding his dish to the stack.

Cassie looked at Grammy. "You said once that your family gave up on the cattle trade because they weren't true farmers. Well, I'm not certain we're true hunters."

Braden started to say something but she held up her hand.

"Hear me out. We all have talents we aren't utilizing here to make additional revenue. I'll help take over the books so Callum can make and sell more furniture. Daddy can think more about those ewes. Billie and Grammy can start selling some of their specialties—pies and jam and ice cream. We could have our own roadside stand at the edge of our property. Maybe even sell syrup beginning of next year."

Billie shared a small smile with me.

"You really think that's going to work?" Braden said.

"How do we know unless we try?" Cassie shrugged. "Braden, you can still run the shooting range and hunting groups, you're good at it. We can all pitch in keeping our land thriving."

"As long as Daddy agrees to take it easy." I gave him a pointed look and he nodded grudgingly. "But maybe it's time to think outside the box."

"So you plan on coming home after graduation?" Daddy said, squeezing Cassie's hand across the table. "I thought I might've lost my daughter to the city."

"I wasn't sure, to be honest, but these new ideas excite me," she said. "And I can still find a course to teach in some university around here."

"Does this have anything to do with a certain boy who runs a fruit stand?" Grammy said, her eyes gleaming.

"Maybe," Cassie said, winking.

Later that evening, Cassie joined me with a beer out on the porch swing. I was gazing up at the sky remembering Dean's excitement over the stars.

"How about you drive back with me in a couple of weeks?" she said, tucking her legs beneath her thighs.

"What do you mean?" I said, my heart thumping a staccato beat.

"Dean would love to have you visit for a weekend," she said, drumming her fist on my knee.

"Wouldn't that just make it tougher?" I asked, my mind a giant cluttered puzzle.

"I don't know, that's up to you guys," she said. "But you're not the only one suffering."

"Yeah?" I said and then bit my lip, trying to keep that fleeting hope at bay.

She shoved at my shoulder playfully. "Of course not."

"I just figured he'd find somebody else," I said, picking at the hem of my jeans. "It's much easier in the city."

"You think it's simple to meet somebody special?" she asked, clucking her tongue at me. "It doesn't matter if the pool is crowded, that one person will always stand out."

My heart rose to my throat. "What would I tell Daddy?"

"That you're checking up on your sister," Grammy said, joining us on the porch with some sweet tea in a tall glass. "And figuring out your future along the way."

31

DEAN

"He'll be here in like ten minutes, Felix," I said.

I saw Felix more when I earned my undergraduate degree at TSU. But that had been more than two years ago and since I moved southeast to earn my master's we'd only been able to talk by phone. Though he planned on visiting next month when he drove through town on some annual motorcycle rally in Laconia.

"You sound nervous as shit," Felix said. "You must really like the guy."

"I do," I said. *More* than like I wanted to say. "But I don't see how we can make it work living in two different states."

"Please, if you both want it..." Felix said. "Look at Smoke and Vaughn. They are still going strong."

Felix had told me about an unlikely pairing of this motorcycle recruit and the bartender of The Hog's Den. I guess Smoke even handed in his cut to run a business with him. They had to keep it hidden for months and then finally said screw it. It all sounded clandestine and dangerous and if I was being honest, pretty damn romantic.

"I guess so," I said, trying not to let too much hope surge through me at the prospect.

"Next phone call, I'll tell you about another something-something brewing in the club," he added. "Then you'll really be convinced."

"Sounds juicy," I replied distractedly, glancing at the clock. "Look forward to."

I was pacing now, so damn nervous. I thought about Callum every day the last couple of weeks and my friends were beginning to grow tired of my glum mood. I also missed having Cassie around but I knew she'd be dealing with her own crisis of the heart, since she'd been spending most of her time with Dermot.

But at least she knew she'd be moving home in less than six months. She and Dermot had a shared history and background. Callum and I had none of that, we were flying blind. I just knew how I felt when I talked to him and how my chest now fluttered with the inevitability of seeing him again.

When Callum asked if I'd be okay with him driving home with Cassie for a visit I nearly burst out of my own skin.

Callum in my city. What would he think, what would we do? How would I ever get over him if it all turned to shit?

When the elevator beeped open at the end of the hall I braced myself. I heard them talking, Cassie explaining something about our building, the key was jiggling in the door, and then they stepped inside.

Holy hot damn, I didn't expect to feel this way upon seeing him. He was a ginger giant with his faded denim jeans, scuffed sneakers, and black ball cap. And he was gorgeous. His eyes met mine and held as we stood gaping at each other.

"You two are something else," Cassie remarked, but it was as if she was talking through a tunnel because all I could focus on was him.

Cassie stepped forward to hug me. "Breathe," she whispered in my ear.

"Welcome home," I croaked out. "I've missed you."

I was talking to Cassie, but my gaze was pinned on Callum's and his eyes glittered the sentiment back.

Callum broke our eye contact to scan the apartment, his gaze perusing the worn couch, the kitchen island, and then snagging on the large picture window littered with my dozens of potted plants. A ghost of a smile traced his lips. "You guys have a nice place."

"Thanks," Cassie said. "Dean, take Callum's things and then feed us. We can go out to eat someplace around here."

Cassie strode down the opposite hall to her room with her suitcase rolling behind her, to put her things away, and probably give us privacy as well.

"Hey, you." Callum stepped closer and as soon as his arms enclosed around me I sighed, because it felt goddamn perfect. He was warm and smelled like pine and earth and it brought the memories of the countryside slamming back full force. I actually missed the quiet of the land and the brilliance of the stars. Grammy's cooking and Billie's laughter as well.

"I can't believe you're here," I mumbled into his neck. "So happy to see you."

He nodded into the top of my hair as we stood hugging for what felt like an eternity, given our stolen moments at the preserve.

"So, hey, let me take your things," I said, dragging myself away and finally getting myself together.

"Where will I be sleeping?" he asked, as I picked up his bag. He worried his lip between his teeth, looking more vulnerable and younger than I'd ever seen him. "I didn't um, want to ask Cassie, exactly."

Never had I been gladder that Cassie and I were on opposite ends of this apartment until now. Well, there'd also been the times either one or the other of us had brought people home. We had a standing rule to play the television or radio at bedtime when guests were over and I hoped she remembered that agreement tonight.

"You're staying in my room," I said, sheepishly. "Hope that's okay."

His eyes blazed and his lips parted. He'd never had the opportunity to be out in the open in quite this way, so I knew how huge this was for him.

"Wow," he breathed out, his eyes darting around the apartment and then back to Cassie's room, maybe having the same thoughts I'd had earlier about privacy.

"What?" I asked, amused by watching him.

"So we really can just be ourselves?" The inflection in his voice made me smile.

I nodded, taking his hand, and walking him down to my room. I was nearly embarrassed at how plain the space was but it was my makeshift home for now. Whereas his room at the ranch was lavish, mine looked almost threadbare because I figured I was only going to be here for a couple of years. Unless I got that full-time lab position.

I set his bag on the desk chair and turned to him. He looked me up and down zeroing in on my T-shirt that read, Let Us All Pause For a Moment of Science.

"You had that on the first day we met," he said, sliding his fingers along the hem and tugging me forward.

"I did," I said, flattered that he'd remembered. "My friend Tate creates his own screen-print designs and has a ton of funny sayings. He made Cassie one for her business major. He's pretty talented."

He was close enough now to gather my face in his hands. It felt like so long since I'd tasted him. His tongue traced my mouth and then slashed past my lips. I moaned into his kiss, grabbing hold of his neck, and drawing him even closer.

"I've been dreaming about that mouth," he said once we broke apart.

"Same," I said, breathless, as I laid my head on his chest.

"Guys, if you want me to get some food by myself I can," Cassie said from the hall. "But if you're going to join me, let's head out now."

We broke apart and grinned. "I forget how cranky she gets when she's starving."

"Feels strange," he said, reaching for the doorknob. "To not have anybody care if you're making out behind closed doors with your boyfriend." His eyes grew wide. "Sorry, didn't mean it that way..."

"No worries," I said against his shoulder blades as I hugged him from behind. "Besides, I like the sound of that."

32

DEAN

Walking out the door, we bypassed Callum's truck. They had made the trek northeast together, but Callum would be heading back alone in a couple days' time.

We pointed out the quaint neighborhood and shopping area, before finally stepping inside one of our favorite eateries, Grub's Diner.

Callum's eyes widened at the large chalkboard menu, seemingly overwhelmed by the large variety of choices. I knew he felt out of his element and that made my stomach drop.

"Your best bet would probably be the mac and cheese," I said, pointing up at the selection while simultaneously placing my hand on the small of his back. He stiffened as his gaze darted around the restaurant. Nobody gave us a second glance but that didn't mean he was ready for any type of public affection. One thing at a time.

When I removed my fingers, his shoulders relaxed. We sat down on three stools at the noisy counter, and our knees brushed as Callum turned to glance out onto the street and then to the tables and chairs lined up along the wall. He certainly got plenty of admiring looks from both men and women and it felt electric having him there with me.

"I felt the same way a couple of years ago," Cassie said after we had placed our orders, and she watched her brother taking all of it in. "Like, how can I ever figure out city life when I'm such a country girl?"

"Yeah, well, it's not like I can live any other place than the preserve," he said as a cloak of gloom settled around us.

"I know you can't see it, Callum," she said, her lips drawn in a grim line. "But you do have choices. You can do whatever you want."

"You know I won't leave Billie," he said and Cassie's gaze softened.

I kept my mouth shut, listening intently, because this was a conversation between brother and sister. I had never considered that Callum might feel trapped. He seemed to enjoy his home and work life. But maybe everybody had something they were fighting against. And for Callum that might've simply been feeling comfortable in his own skin. It had taken me years to accomplish that, so I knew he needed time to reconcile everything.

"I'll be back soon enough," she said. "But ten years down the line, what if Daddy is gone and Grammy too? Braden will be there, but he might be married. Me too. Even Billie. What then?"

"I don't know," he said, bracing his jaw. "I can't plan that far ahead. But I like your ideas about the preserve. I'm excited about working in the sawmill again."

"It's what you excel at," she said. "You're good at the business end too, don't get me wrong. But I think you're better suited working with your hands."

"I think she might be right," I said in a quiet voice. "Your craftsmanship is amazing."

I looked down at Callum's large hands splayed on the counter and imagined what he could build with them. I didn't have a creative bone in my body.

"I've always just done what was needed," he said, shrugging. "I've never really given what I wanted much thought."

"Well maybe you should," she said, taking a sip of her soda.

I figured a change of subject was in order before the mood turned even glummer.

"So what kind of movies do you like?" I asked Callum. "There's a few playing at the local cinema."

"We don't have a theatre in town," he said, his shoulders slumping. "I catch some good action flicks on the television sometimes." He played with his straw, as if we had reached an impasse. But I was determined to show him that we had more in common than he realized.

"I don't go much either, honestly," I said and his eyes sprang back to mine. "I like staying home and renting movies. Sometimes I can get Cassie to watch a television series with me."

"Like what?" Callum asked, the corner of his mouth lifting into a pained smile.

"Like the Walking Dead," Cassie said, dryly. "But I have to cover my face a lot. The suspense kills me more than the gore."

"You never did like those kind of shows," Callum said, shaking his head. "I'm almost caught up to season four actually, so don't spoil anything for me."

I knew we'd meet someplace in the middle and I was so relieved, I reached for his fingers beneath the counter and he gave my hand a gentle squeeze.

Just then, the door flew open and in walked my friend Tate, with a guy I'd seen around campus with him before.

Tate was a lean, good-looking guy who always wore bright colors. Today his hair had streaks of blue and his rainbow tie-dyed shirt read, I'm Not Gay, But My Boyfriend Is, in bold black letters.

"Dean," Tate called across the room.

He and his friend approached and Tate gave Cassie and me hugs. I could tell the instant Callum read his handmade T-shirt. His eyebrows shot up and a blush stole across his cheeks.

"Who's your friend?" Tate asked, approvingly. I knew that Callum was Tate's type because he pursued tall, muscular guys and his claim to fame was seducing a couple of supposedly straight men. I warned him that one day some guy was going to sweep him off his feet and he would be done for. But he always laughed it off because he loved flirting and playing the field.

"Tate, meet my brother Callum," Cassie said, turning in her seat, an amused glint in her eye.

"So this is the infamous Callum?" Tate made a sweeping gesture and Callum's gaze darted around the room in mortification.

"Nice to meet you." Callum held out his hand like a true Southern gentleman.

"You are one fine looking man," Tate said, gripping his hand a little too long for my taste. "No wonder Dean is all aflutter about his ginger boy."

Callum's face practically turned as flaming red as his hair and his eyes flashed to mine.

"Is that right?" Callum asked out of the corner of his mouth.

I rolled my eyes at my friend. "Tate likes to exaggerate a bit."

"Oh, please," Tate continued and even narrowing my eyes in warning wouldn't dissuade him. "For weeks it's been Callum this and Callum *that*. He doesn't even give other guys a second glance."

I was used to Tate's insanity but for Callum's sake, thank fuck our food arrived just then. In another minute I was going to knee my loudmouth friend in the nuts.

"I'll let you get to eating," Tate said, pulling out his wallet to place a to-go order at the counter. "How long will you be in town?"

"Just for the weekend," Callum said, eyeing his heaping bowl of mac and cheese.

"Will you guys meet us at The Nickel tomorrow night?" Tate asked as his friend wandered off to speak to somebody he noticed across the room.

My gaze met Callum's. "Only if Callum wants to."

"Sounds fine to me," Callum said, lifting his fork to jab at the charred edges of cheese.

Cassie was already scarfing down her sandwich as we turned in our seats to eat. We tasted our food in virtual silence, all of us apparently starving.

"It's really delicious," Callum said after another minute and several more bites.

I nodded, crunching on a piece of crushed ice from my soda. "So how's my sugar cane field holding up?"

"Grammy's thrilled about it," Callum said. "Overheard her talking to Daddy about making syrup again."

"That would be amazing," I said. "I've been asking around the lab, actually."

"You still talking to Professor Landon from my old alma mater?" he asked. "His class was one of my favorites."

"He's a great guy." I was glad to have gotten his business card at the county fair because he was actually a fascinating study in farming and herbology. "He's given me some suggestions for when the plants are finally budding above ground."

"Billie has sort of taken the project under his wing," Cassie said. "He begged to come with us this weekend."

I imagined Billie and Bullseye walking along the city streets. I think he'd love it and I wished I could help expand his worldview, but I needed to stay away from making any promises I couldn't keep. "Tell me how he's doing."

"Pretty well," Cassie said. "He's been getting more sleep and hasn't had any repeat incidents."

"How about the rest of your family?" I asked. "Especially since you came out to them?"

"It's taken some adjustment from my dad and Braden," Callum said. "But the other day at the shooting range, Braden told me that so much makes sense now. Said my being honest has given him the gumption to finally break up with Jennifer."

After we paid our bill and headed out the door, I said, "So what do you want to do next?"

"You guys figure it out," Cassie said. "I'll catch up with you at the house. Laundry is calling me."

33

CALLUM

Being in the city was sort of like being in a foreign country. I didn't know if I fit in here and I sure as hell felt like I stuck out like a sore thumb.

The way my sister and Dean maneuvered around their neighborhood made me feel like I was extra weight that needed to get dumped overboard.

I knew the preserve, could navigate the land with my eyes closed. It was noisy here, crowded in certain areas. Exciting at times, like it had a pulse of its own, but I missed the quieter moments. The sound of the wind as it whistled around the pines, the trickle of the creek, the squawking of birds in flight.

Even the food had fancy combinations. But it tasted good. Dean kept asking me if I was okay. At times he looked disappointed. Did he hope I'd be so taken with the hum and cadence of this lively town that I'd consider moving? That was why this—whatever this was between us—never stood a chance. It was wiser to simply enjoy the time we had together in the here and now.

Except even in the swell of the crowd, when Dean's hand connected briefly with mine, everything became crystal clear, like it was obvious, meant to be. Some folks looked our way, but by and large nobody seemed to care. They were too busy getting where they needed to go.

When Dean showed me his university lab, I was in awe. He placed those sexy black frames on his eyes to read through one of the slides before we were on our way again. I looked around the room, wanting to grab him and throw him up on the counter, but I kept myself composed.

Dean could read my body language, he remembered my fantasy, and he teased me mercilessly. Brushing past my hip to grab something from the drawer, he smirked.

"Just you wait," I said, under my breath.

"I look forward to it," he murmured close by my ear.

As soon as we were back in the empty elevator, I attacked his mouth, forcing him against the wall for two brief floors until the door dinged open.

"You okay with going home now?" Dean asked as we waited at the crosswalk. "I just want to spend time alone with you."

My pulse kicked up. "I want that too."

As we headed toward his apartment, we paused along the edge of a small park to watch an inning of a little league game. In the country, games were a huge draw for folks. But here, the stands were empty, probably only filled with family members.

"What position did you play in high school?" Dean asked, watching a small kid in a red uniform throw a pitch.

"I was an outfielder," I said. "Was also a power hitter. Usually fourth in the lineup."

"I could see that." He slid his fingers around my bicep, which was flexed from grasping onto the fence.

"But you never wanted to pursue it?" Dean asked. "Beyond school?"

"Nah, wasn't *that* good," I said. "To be honest, I was so ready for the season to be over my senior year."

"I'm confused," he said, meeting my eyes. "I thought you enjoyed it."

"I did. But I..." Clearing my throat, I felt a line of heat crawl across my neck. "I was really hung up on our star pitcher. It was torture in the locker room, at team outings..."

"Why would it be...?" Dean's eyes became wide. "Okay, got it. That's when you first figured out you were gay?"

"Right," I said, wincing. "And I had no idea what to do with those feelings. So I just stuffed them. Guess in a lot of ways, I still don't know. But I'm working on it."

Dean's mouth stretched into this gorgeous and seductive grin. I didn't know what came over me but I leaned over and pecked his lips.

When a startled gasp released from his mouth, I looked around the street, having totally forgotten myself. Nobody had pitchforks ready to skewer us. In fact, nobody had given us a second glance.

"Feels good, doesn't it?" Dean whispered.

"Yeah," I said, releasing my breath.

We ordered Chinese food for dinner, a delicacy I hadn't eaten since I was commuting to college a few years back. I even sampled Dean's tofu, which was spicy and pretty decent.

We ate in the living room with Cassie, who turned on some romantic comedy that I could barely concentrate on; I wanted so badly to be touching Dean.

We retired to bed early and lay naked in his sheets, facing each other. "I can't wrap my head around not having to hide or rush."

"Honestly, I was afraid it would take away the mystique for you," Dean said, not meeting my eyes. "Maybe this weekend you'd realize I was only some regular guy you weren't even inter- ested in any more, in a whole city of regular guys."

"No way. Would it help to know that I was plenty nervous myself?" I asked. "That you'd return to the city and realize you have an ample supply of men to choose from, without the headache of being attracted to some closeted gay guy?"

"But it doesn't work that way. I thought about you constantly." His eyes latched on to mine. "I'm so drawn to you, can barely take my eyes off of you. Feel all kinds of things having you here."

I shifted to lie on top of him, our groins lining up with no barriers between us. It felt so fucking perfect. "Do you even know how sexy you are and how badly I need to kiss you?"

His eyelashes fluttered and his hands glided down the column of my spine. "Then kiss me already."

My mouth feathered over Dean's lips as I watched him. His reactions to me. His breath caught in his throat and he stared back with so much longing it made my cock stiffen painfully.

I licked into his mouth and deepened the kiss, my fingers clutching at his hair and holding him right against my mouth. Right where I needed him.

We kissed until our lips were bruised, Dean's hands exploring my skin, rubbing over my thighs and ass until I was leaking across his stomach. His hands grabbed at my cheeks and split them apart, his fingers running along my crease as I gasped into his mouth.

"I've missed your cock," Dean said, tugging at my thighs, urging me to straddle his chest. "Let me lick you."

My knees landed on either side of his neck, my cock stabbing at his lips, dribbling come down his chin. He shoved two digits in his mouth, getting them nice and wet.

When his finger penetrated my hole, I groaned. His tongue darted out to lick around the crown before he suckled on my head. My fingers carded through his hair and clutched tight when he took more of me inside all that heat.

"Fuck my mouth," he said around my girth. When he plunged a second finger inside me, I arched my neck and drove to the back of his throat. Saliva leaked out the side of his mouth and feeling him hum around me was almost too much to bear.

When his other hand stretched up to tweak my nipple, I almost came right then.

"Goddamn. Wait," I ground out, dragging my cock from his mouth. "I need. I can't..."

Dean gripped my thighs, his mouth swollen from sucking me. "Fuck me, please. I don't want to wait anymore."

Our eyes met and held. He shifted, turning over on his belly as he reached for the condoms he had placed on his bedside table. He lifted up on his knees, his ass in the air to stretch to the far side for the lube and I couldn't wait any longer to have him.

I grabbed his cheeks, split them open, and dove straight in.

Dean gasped as my tongue licked at his hole. "Mmmmmm..."

He squirmed barely able to stay still as I continued to kiss and suck around the muscled rim, attempting to wiggle my tongue inside.

"Damn. Hold on." Dean's limbs stiffened, his neck bowed back, and he collapsed to the mattress groaning.

I slid behind him in bed, wrapping my arms around his chest, my cock skimming along his crease. I could feel all of his naked skin against me and I wasn't sure if I would even last being inside him.

"Please," Dean choked out. "Need you now."

I tore apart the condom wrapper with my teeth and folded it down my length. Opening the lube, I slicked my cock and then two of my fingers to push inside him. He moaned and drove his ass against my hand.

Finally, I lifted his knee toward his stomach and pressed my length forward. I ground my teeth with restraint and stabbed at his hole, the head of my cock finally breaching him.

My breath whooshed from my lungs and my eyesight fuzzed as I attempted to harness the intense carnal pleasure that whirred through all of my nerve endings at once, catching them on fire.

"Oh fuck," Dean mumbled into the pillow. "Give me a second."

"Am I hurting you?" I asked, clearing the fog from my head, ready to pull out.

"Don't you dare," Dean said, his fingers biting into my thigh. "I just... you're so thick... But I want you. *Please*."

I took a deep breath and surged forward again. Fuck, so *tight*. It was hard not to pound him into the mattress except this position made that prospect difficult. But our bodies were pasted together, I was breathing into his neck, and I had never felt closer to him.

I rounded my hand over his hip to his cock, which was stiff and heavy against his stomach.

As my hand slicked over his length, I pumped my hips in shallow thrusts, clenching my jaw, as small licks of flames sparked up my spine.

"Oh God, that's—" Dean was huffing, arching his back, his nipples were hard, and his fingers were trembling as he slid them over my hand.

"You feel incredible." I bit and sucked on the skin between his shoulder and neck. "But I need to be facing you. I want to see your eyes when you break apart for me."

Dean was so far gone he couldn't even respond, only groaned and adjusted himself to his back after I pulled out my cock. As I hovered over him, I hiked his knees to his shoulders. His eyes latched onto mine, I situated his ankles around my neck and plunged back inside, stealing his breath along with mine.

"*Uuuhhh*." The sensation of being inside him again from this position was like a cold punch to my chest. "Goddamn."

Dean kept his gaze on me, his trembling hand reaching up to outline my lips. I sucked his finger into my mouth and traced it with my tongue. He closed his eyes and sighed.

When he opened his lids his irises were a poignant blue, like a cloudless sky, as they reached inside and dragged me to the heavens. "Need you. Need *more*."

"Fuck." I could hear our flesh slapping together as I slammed into Dean with a demanding pace. His fingers tightened in the covers, his sobs becoming hoarse. I forced his hips upward to change the angle and watching his ass stretch around my length only spurred me on.

I was so deep and striking that spongy place inside him that was driving him wild.

His eyes widened, his moans harsh and keening right before he sprayed his load all over his stomach. His ass constricted almost painfully tight around my cock and I was ricocheted into the atmosphere right along with him.

"Dean," I murmured, collapsing on top of him and in that moment it was as if we had no hurdles between us, no distance. We were one, living and breathing in unison.

It was so seamless. Profound. Right.

34

CALLUM

Dean was still in my arms, in an actual bed, and it felt so damn good that I didn't want to move.

I had stirred in the middle of the night and felt his hips squirm seductively against mine, so without another word, I clumsily slid on a condom, and stuffed my cock back inside him.

I urged Dean flat on his stomach and ground into him in slow rhythmic moves. Our breaths were harsh and our moans were in sync, as we came one after the other. I remained in that position, my cock buried deep in his ass, my forehead resting against his shoulder blades, simply enjoying the idea that I could stay connected to him for as long as I pleased.

By the time I pulled out and reached for a shirt to clean us both up, Dean was fast asleep again, so I just slipped into his warm bed and passed out.

"Want to go running with me?" Dean mumbled.

"Sure," I said. "Just lie here for five more minutes?"

He threw his leg over mine, his face at my neck, as he settled back in the sheets.

Just as my breathing was beginning to even out again, he whispered, "Let's go before the city wakes up."

"Why?" I mumbled.

"It's more peaceful that way." His answer surprised me, allowing a sliver of hope to slip momentarily inside. I wondered if he missed the serenity of the preserve and would consider visiting again.

But then what? Long distance was rough especially if there wasn't a common future goal. Dean had never said he'd want to move anywhere closer to me and it was selfish on my part, because I couldn't leave my home. Not when Billie was there, when Grammy was getting up in age, when my daddy hoped to pass on the land to his children one day.

Ten minutes more and we slipped out the door into the dusk morning. Dean loaned me some baggy shorts and a T-shirt that pulled too tight across my shoulders. But they smelled like him and that brought me a quiet comfort.

Some of the corner lamps were still lit and added a charm to the concrete sidewalks and cobblestone streets that I hadn't detected in the drone of the crowd. Right away I noticed the different sounds of the city. Engines revving from early risers. Store owners rolling up their security doors and dragging out heavy signs and displays. A couple of them waved to Dean and looked curiously at me.

By now the gossip would be abundant back home at Sunnyside Up Diner, but out here I suspected we were forgotten as soon as our sneakers rounded the corner. That kind of anonymity was appealing, if not unsettling in its disregard for human connections. It was a strange paradox that only scrambled my brain further.

We slowed to a walk on our way back, as I held my fingers against the stitch in my side, Dean's sweat-soaked T-shirt clinging more snugly to my skin.

At a shop around the corner from his place, we stopped for coffee. He placed Cassie's order, adding three breakfast sandwiches, and I pictured this being their daily routine. They embraced the city in a way that we didn't on the preserve.

We used the resources of our land, much like they relied on the local amenities to get their basic needs met in their neighborhood. In that regard, there was more of a sense of community than I had first anticipated.

We sat at the kitchen island eating our organic egg sandwiches and drinking our strong coffee. Cassie was bleary eyed and chuckled at us for getting up so early on a weekend.

"My roommate's corrupted you," she said with a gleam in her eye and I had to wonder if she heard us last night. "I thought you'd want to sleep in."

Dean gave me a lingering kiss in front of Cassie before he strolled off to shower. I had a hard time meeting her eyes, but she seemed nonplussed, which I was grateful for.

"You glad to be back?" I mumbled into my recycled cup.

"It's bittersweet," Cassie said. "It's nice to know you can make it on your own, but you still miss home."

Though it wasn't her intent, her words socked me in the gut. Would I ever be able to make it on my own? I knew the thought was ridiculous in many ways, because I'd helped run a large piece of land since I was a teen.

But I also lived with my relatives and only now came out of the closet. I used to dream about building a home someday. Not to get away from my family, but to have something to call my own.

Not an actual house, though there would be room for that on our property. Something more the size of a trailer. A couple of years back, Daddy and I had erected the frame of a small place on the other side of the orchard, about eight hundred square feet. But I had abandoned the idea when we got busy.

"What are you going to do about Dermot?" I asked.

"We'll continue to talk and visit each other," she said, dreamily. "I've only got five months until I move back home."

My gut tightened. They had a plan, something Dean and I skirted around, because there didn't seem to be an easy resolution. In Cassie and Dermot's case, they came from the same small town and knew each other from school. Cassie was happy to return to living and working with her family. There was little to decide.

Dean was a city boy and I was a country boy. Though he hinted at times of things he loved about a quieter life, it was nearly delusional to imagine him making that kind of jump.

"What happens to this apartment?" I asked, looking around at the mish-mash of shared furniture.

"Dean and I will have to figure that out," she said. "If he stays at his job, he'll have to find a roommate, unless the pay is good."

I imagined some hot guy responding to his ad in the newspaper, moving in with him, and I felt bile crawl up my throat.

"Can you see yourself living here?" Cassie asked in a tentative voice, as if I'd bite her head off.

"No," I said. "It feels impossible. But I..."

"You're in love with him."

I inhaled a sharp breath. It had probably been written all over my face and I wondered now if Dean saw it too, what he did to me. How he made me feel so completely twisted inside out.

"Hell, is it that obvious?" I asked as my chest felt impossibly crowded. "I wish I weren't. I don't like this ache, this longing I have. It's painful."

"He's going through the same thing," she said. "Maybe you should tell him how you feel."

I shook my head. "I don't want to make it worse. Or leave him feeling guilty. He needs to make his own decisions."

I drove to the university bookstore with Dean in his used Mazda sedan, the same one he'd brought down to the preserve. It felt cramped in his small interior not only because I was tall but probably because I was used to the truck or van. We purchased his books together for his final class, and though

Dean was only three years younger, I felt old in this campus setting.

Dean said as much about himself when we got back in the car to drive someplace for a late lunch. "I know I'll probably always be in the academia setting, given my degree, but it'll be nice to not be a student anymore."

"I don't think you could pay me to return to school," I said as I reached for his hand and settled into the seat. I looked out the window at the passing landscape and asked the question I was scared to admit I needed to know. "Do you like this city?"

He looked from my eyes down to my mouth, where my bottom lip was enclosed between my teeth. "You do that when you're anxious."

"Do what?" I said, licking at my tender mouth.

He motioned with his hand. "You bite your lip when something's bothering you."

I fumbled for a response, so taken with the fact that Dean could read me so well in such a short period of time.

"Yeah? Well you get all brainy on me," I said, twirling my finger. "You spout off some facts about this, that, and the other. At the beginning I thought you were just some know it all. But then I realized you were only nervous."

"Because you like to challenge me," he said with a smirk. "And right now you're searching for an answer to make sense of what it is that we're doing. And I'm not sure I have one. Not yet."

I dropped his hand, but he grabbed for it again and held it firmly in his own. "And now you're being stubborn."

"I'm not being—"

"You're disappointed," he said, reading me perfectly. "The reason I don't have an answer is because it depends on where a job will lead me."

"I only asked if you liked this city," I threw out. "I wasn't trying to get you to admit to anything else."

"Okay," he said, dismissing my argument, as if he didn't

believe a lick of what I was saying. "I enjoy city life, sure. This one had a lot to offer. But right now my mind is on graduating and finding a decent job. You're lucky in that regard. You know what you want to do and you have a huge support system."

"Fair enough," I said, regretting that I even asked the question. I didn't want us to fight when I was only here for a couple of days. I had forgotten that his family wasn't as involved and encouraging as he would've liked them to be and that bummed me out.

He was only trying to make something of himself. But damn it, I wanted to be his rock, his support, no matter how ridiculous that sounded at this stage of the game.

Just then my phone beeped with a text from Billie.

Tell Dean I checked on his sugar canes and all looks good. But he better come back for a visit to see for himself.

I relayed the message to Dean, who smiled. "Tell him I miss him and that I'll plan a trip after I graduate in a couple of months."

My heart clanked against my ribcage. I couldn't help feeling optimistic that there was a chance of seeing him again.

And the way he tenderly held my hand through our intimate lunch in a booth at some swanky diner, I got the feeling that maybe he felt the exact same way.

35

CALLUM

Cassie had a Rascal Flatts concert she was attending with a group of campus classmates at the Greensboro Coliseum, which was one of the reasons she had driven back from the preserve early.

She had kissed each of our cheeks, reminding us she'd be home late because of the distance, but that she'd check in with us later.

I had agreed to meet Dean's friends at a gay bar tonight and I'd admit I was sort of nervous. Not because of the club. I had been to a few out of the way places over the years with Jason and sometimes by myself. But if his friend Tate was any indication, the men in these places were worldlier and definitely livelier.

But I'd been wrong upon entering The Nickel, which I soon realized was a nickname for an establishment called The Five Cent that more resembled a dive bar. It was dim and unobtrusive, much like you'd see at any corner pub in any city, upon first glance.

The tables were full and there was music playing in the background. Men were talking, laughing, eating, and some were even dancing and making out.

When we walked in all eyes seemed to zero in on me, like the bullseye in the center of a dartboard. I tensed and almost released Dean's hand, but he interlaced our fingers making sure to hold on tight.

"It's all good," Dean said. "Just...you know, new kid on the block."

My eyes widened and darted to his as his lips swung close to my ear.

"Meaning—dude, you are so hot, everyone will want to hook up with you," he said in a low murmur.

"That's too bad," I said, against his neck. "Because I only want to be with you."

His gaze blazed with affection. "You realize I'm the envy of this place, right?"

"I don't get it." I shrugged. "I'm just a hick from out of town."

"Who just happens to be drop dead gorgeous," Dean said, motioning with his hands. "And has a cocky swagger."

"I do not," I scoffed, shoving my other hand in my pocket, as some very attractive man with dark hair and skin made eyes at me.

"Do too," he said, arching his eyebrow. "Think of when we first met. All that macho bravado. So hot."

I shook my head, heat climbing up my neck. I knew he was just messing around but hearing him call me hot and gorgeous did all kinds of things to me.

I had the blinding urge to fuck him right here in the middle of the club. Which either made me kinky as hell or so into Dean, I didn't give a shit who knew it right then.

Dean lifted his chin at the bartender, who was pierced, tattooed, and sporting spiky blond hair.

"Haven't seen you in a long minute," the bartender said. "What can I get for you and your friend?"

He looked me up and down appreciatively but was discreet about it.

"You cool with whatever they have on draft?" Dean asked, as he eyed the selection of brews.

"Sounds good," I said, not really particular about my booze.

"This is your first time here since you've been back?" I asked, as we waited for our drinks, not sure if I wanted to hear the answer.

"Yep," he said, nodding to a couple of men he recognized sitting on bar stools.

"I guess I just thought you'd—" I let out a breath. "I don't know."

"What?" he asked, angling his head toward me. "You thought I'd run out and get laid?"

I looked down at my feet, embarrassed for even asking. "Yeah, suppose so."

Dean gripped my neck and planted a wet kiss on my lips. "Did you really think I could fuck you out of my system? Not a chance."

I slid my fingers beneath his jaw and stared into his eyes. It was as if everything else fell away in that moment—the drone of the music and the conversations around us. The stares of the other patrons seated near us. There was warmth and affection in Dean's gaze and all I could think was that I had placed it there.

Me. Some redneck from a hunting preserve.

There were plenty of hot men in this bar. Dean could have his fill of any one of them. Men who were probably academics like him, liberal minded, and intelligent. Men who could rock his world.

But he was choosing me. At least for tonight.

Dean never broke his gaze, his fingers bracing my waist, until the bartender slid our tall glasses of beer toward us. Dean paid before I even had the chance to retrieve my wallet and in the next second we were toasting and sipping our drinks.

A couple of guys were waving from the back of the room, attempting to gain our attention, and I recognized Tate immediately. Not because of his blue hair, but because he was wearing glittery eyelashes, lipstick, and a large cocktail ring on his finger. He was definitely a pretty boy, mesmerizing really, and I wondered if he ever dressed in full drag. Given his charisma, he would probably have a large following if he ever took the stage.

"Uh, those must be your friends," I said and Dean grabbed for my hand and headed their way.

There were three more men seated at their table, all of them handsome in their own way, and they shook my hand as Dean made his introductions.

"See, didn't I tell you Callum was hot as sin?" Tate said to one of the guys, who smiled and nodded. Tonight he wore a T-shirt that read, Biggest Lesbian In the Room.

"Just ignore him," another dude named Stephen said. His long eyelashes fluttered and framed his brown eyes in an enticing way.

"I'm only being honest," Tate said, jutting out his lower lip, as he looked me up and down. "Bet Callum makes a fantastic top."

I felt my cheeks flame hot. But I had nothing to be ashamed of, if anything I should finally feel free to talk openly in a roomful of gay men. It would just take some getting used to.

"Rein it in," Dean said, throwing him a death glare.

"Nah, no worries." I flung my arm around Dean's shoulders. "I actually love to bottom, too. I'm hoping my boy here hooks me up tonight."

The other guys whistled as Dean's eyes flared. His mouth split into a wide grin and I felt like I had broken the ice a bit.

"Is that true?" Dean whispered in my ear, after we sat down in a couple of high-back chairs at the table. "You want me to fuck you sometime?"

I kissed his cheek, my mouth going dry, even imagining the prospect. "Damn, now you've got me hard, thinking about your cock in my ass. Does that answer your question?"

Dean swore under his breath and reached for my hand,

tugging it to his lap, so I could feel the boner he was sporting. He teased me mercilessly by keeping my hand there as he talked to his friends across the table about their summer jobs or classes.

I swallowed roughly thinking about anything else besides sex with Dean—like how crowded this place must really get when fall term was back in session.

"So Tate says you live on a farm?" Stephen asked across the table and I felt like the outsider all over again. Dean squeezed my fingers to either support me or temper me, I wasn't sure which. But if it was the latter, I didn't appreciate it very much. Sure, I could be grumpy, but I knew how to use my manners out in public.

"Not exactly. It's a hunting preserve and I help run it with my family," I said, cringing at having to reveal that hot button word. I hoped nobody tried to challenge me on guns and animal cruelty. Though I stood by my beliefs and could even bust some of the lamer myths, I was not in the mood tonight. "We only keep chickens, and the rest of the animals are free to live off the land as they see fit."

When Stephen only nodded and then began talking to one of the other guys about something in the local news, I relaxed against the seat.

And after another beer, I was feeling pretty comfortable in this crowd.

The music got louder, the bass more frenetic, and a number of men jumped up to dance to the techno beat. Dean asked if I was interested in getting my groove on but I swore him off. This kind of music usually just made my teeth clatter and gave me a headache.

"You go," I said, grinning. "I'll watch."

I sipped on my beer as Dean swayed his hips with a group of men in the middle of the floor. He looked sexy as hell and when he began dirty dancing with a couple of the guys from the table, my dick swelled. It was fucking hot and maybe if he had allowed some strangers to grope him, I would've been jealous, but these were his friends and they were only having a good time.

"I bet you feel like a kid in a candy store here," Tate said, sidling up beside me.

"What do you mean?" I asked, as he rapped his knuckles in time to the beat.

"You can have your pick of anybody in this bar." I looked around the room and saw that several eyes were indeed honing in on me.

I guess he might be right. I could go home with anybody I supposed. But that just wasn't in my blood. I'd picked up men in bars before and even though I got my rocks off, it also felt pretty empty driving back home alone.

"Too bad I only want one person here," I said, after sipping from the bottom of my glass.

His brow quirked and his gaze followed mine to the dance floor.

"You got it bad for Dean, huh?" he asked.

I shrugged. "Guess I do."

"Dean's had his share of flings but never something like this. The way he acts around you is different." His eyes darted away with something that looked like remorse. "Wish I knew how you guys could make it work."

I wasn't expecting that response from him. He seemed so flippant and lively and happy-go-lucky. But maybe he had loved and lost as well.

"Me too," I mumbled but I wasn't even sure he could hear me over the buzz of the crowd.

The lights dimmed and the music changed to a slower tempo. Dean hooked his fingers, motioning for me to join him. A few of the couples were already lip locked and grinding on each other.

I stood and made my way past swaying twosomes to get to him. He grabbed my hand, swinging it around his back, which was sticky with moisture from gyrating his hips the past hour.

"I wanted to dance with you at the wedding. So here's my chance," he said. "Though it would've been so much better underneath the moon."

"Yeah?" I murmured, allowing my hope to surge again.

"Who could resist that setting?" he said, sinking into my embrace. I tightened my hold on his waist as his arms glided around my neck.

I could smell his grapefruit shampoo and when his lips brushed against my chin I sighed.

His wet kisses traveled to my ear and then across my jawline. When our mouths met, it was just like that first time at Pines Ledge. My heart was pounding out of my chest, Dean's skin gleamed with a sheen of sweat, and I could've sworn I'd never tasted sweeter lips.

Even tonight as his tongue licked inside my mouth with a mix of mint and salt and beer, I didn't want to be anywhere else in the world except right next to him.

36

DEAN

"We can leave any time you want," I said into Callum's neck, smelling him, tasting his skin. It felt so good having him here, even though I knew he felt out of sorts. What he didn't realize was that if he were just himself, everybody would fall in love with him, same as me. "I only thought you'd want to be in a place where you felt..."

"I appreciate that," he said, resting his forehead against mine. "But a bar is still only a bar. People hanging out, hooking up. It's not always my scene."

"So you don't want to hook up with anybody from this bar?" I asked in a whisper.

His head sprang back. "Hell no."

"Not even me?" I asked coyly.

He tugged my hips flush against his and growled in my ear.

"I want you so bad, you don't even know the half of it," he said, after nipping at my shoulder. "This is your world and I don't know how I fit unless I'm next to you, then it feels..."

"What?" I asked against his lips.

"Feels damn good," he said, kissing me. "Like it all clicks into place."

"Same here." I sighed, my heart feeling like it might burst wide open because I didn't know what to do about this big hunk of man who held me securely in his arms.

The thing I said to him earlier in the car about not knowing where my job would lead me was true. But it was also for his benefit because he only recently came out and maybe he needed to explore his newfound status a bit more. Get off the preserve and see what it's all about, not be chained to text messages from me.

Right then Tate headed over to us, and nudged at my arm playfully.

"I'm about to hook up with some dude. Says he's at The Nickel tonight." He held out his cell to show me the photo he found on the gay app we all used. "He messaged that he's waiting for me at the bar. What do you think?"

I stared at the photo of the buff dude who looked a little too shiny and fake tan for my taste. But he had muscles, which was what Tate liked. "I think you'd go for it no matter what I say. But sure, go meet him."

"You think so, Callum?" he asked shoving the phone in his direction.

Callum's shoulders hunched up as if surprised he'd even asked. "I say yeah, but don't leave with him unless you feel, you know, *safe*."

I wondered if that warning had come because Callum was being particularly cautious about being in the city, or if something had happened once to somebody he knew.

"He looks like a teddy bear farm boy like you," Tate said, twirling his finger. "Should be okay."

Callum watched as Tate walked away and I had trouble reading his body language. His face has become a mask, his body rigid.

"A bear is just a type for gays. Tate's kind for sure," I said, placing my hand on his shoulder. "And there's this app you can use on your smart phone to meet people in your own city when you're out—"

Callum took a step back and snorted out a laugh. "Really?"

"What?" My eyebrows slammed together. "Why are you—?"

"There you go again, schooling me. Do you really think I'm that naive?" he said, throwing up his hands. "You think I've never heard of Grindr? I've used it to fuck my share of men."

"Callum, I never meant..." I sputtered. "I just thought..."

"You figured us rednecks still used rotary phones or maybe telegrams? Yeah, that's it. We meet in the hayloft and screw next to them stallions in the barn," he said in his best Southern drawl. "Don't be so full of yourself, city boy."

He spun on his heel to leave the dance floor. I attempted to grab hold of his arm. "Where the hell are you going?"

"I think I'm done here." He passed my table of friends and headed toward the exit.

I followed him outside as he strode down the pavement. "What are you going to do, walk home?"

"Maybe I will," he threw over his shoulder, as he turned the corner down some side street the opposite direction of my car. "Or maybe I'll get lost. I've never been without my horse and carriage."

"Will you fucking stop already? I get it, okay? Yeah, I spew off crap." I caught up to him and tugged on his forearm. "And you're not stupid. Fuck, you're smarter than me and you don't even realize it. Maybe you have everything I want and I'm envious of that."

He spun on me, his teeth clamping down. "Envy?"

"That's right," I said, latching onto his fingers. This time he didn't pull away. A couple of people passed by us on the sidewalk, but other than that we were alone—at least momentarily. "You have an amazing family. People who are always in your business, have your back, and love you no matter what. I wish I had a Billie and a Cassie in my life. I wish they were my siblings."

His eyes tempered to swirls of golden amber, but there was still underlying tension and anger in his gaze. "You have parents who—"

"Parents who throw themselves into work and charity events, who won't admit out loud that I'm gay. Who are never around for holidays, because they lost a son, and it's too painful for them," I said, my voice gruff. "Little do they remember I'm the other child who needs those things. I don't have anybody, not really. Not anymore. I'm not part of any kind of family."

"*Fuck.* You listen here," Callum said, stepping forward and shoving me against the brick building. His face buried in my neck. "No matter what happens with us, you can always come to Shady Pines. My family will always welcome you. Cassie and Billie, they...they *love* you."

A muddled word caught in his throat and then he mashed his mouth against mine. A deep and bruising kiss that leaked into my heart and stained my soul.

He snatched my hands, lifting them above my head, as he crushed his body against mine, enclosing me in all of that warmth, right there in the middle of the street.

It was the first time I'd witnessed Callum entirely uninhibited in public and it was bittersweet and breathtaking all at once.

His heartbeat was thundering against my chest, his stiff cock rubbing my groin, and I was suspended in some sort of dreamland where none of our differences existed.

When he finally dragged his lips away from mine we were panting heavily into each other's mouths.

"Let's get out of here," I said in a hoarse voice.

He looked around as if only just realizing where the hell we were and what the heck we were doing.

We drove to my apartment in overwhelming silence, hands clasped together, and somehow I just knew deep in my gut that I would never have this again. Not with him.

I didn't know what to say or even feel, I just wanted the heavy weight to be lifted off my chest.

As soon as we were inside the door, we kicked out of our shoes and tore off each other's clothes, leaving a trail of shirts and pants to my room. I'd worry about cleaning up later.

We stumbled onto the bed and he dragged me on top, his tongue in my ear, his teeth along my jaw, his fingers burrowed tightly in my hair.

"Fuck me," he said, his tongue licking into my mouth. "Please fuck me. I need to feel you."

I stared long and hard into his eyes, looking for the underpinning of truth.

"I want to remember exactly how you felt inside me," he huffed against my lips and grabbed my ass to tow my groin firmly against him. "I *need* to remember."

I bit back a moan, despair and longing warring in my chest. I rose up on my elbows, stretching for a condom and lube.

He lifted his knees and spread his legs open for me. And hell, Callum offering himself up to me like that was so damn incredible.

I carelessly slicked my fingers with lube, desperate to feel connected to him. His cock was enflamed and seeping and as I pushed my fingers inside him, he moaned, mashing his head side to side on the pillow.

His knees trembled when I kissed a stripe on the inside of his thigh. He cried out, clutching at the sheets, when I licked around the head of his cock, as I simultaneously pumped my fingers in and out of his ass.

After I rolled on the condom Callum pleaded with his eyes. I slipped my cock against his hole, applying light pressure, wondering if I'd even last.

"Now, Dean," he rasped. "Right fucking now."

Driving inside him in one solid thrust, a fine tremor crackled across my shoulders and down the center of my spine.

"Uuuuhhhhh." A warm flush stained Callum's cheeks, neck,

and chest.

I hissed remaining motionless and attempting not to break apart right then and there.

Callum moaned, arching his back, and reaching for my shoulder to drag me into a messy kiss.

"Does it sting?" I asked against his mouth, as I nipped greedily at his lips.

"Some," he said, his hand quivering as it tightened around my nape, aligning our foreheads. "Don't care. Because it's you."

He sank against the sheets and sighed, his cinnamon eyelashes shuttering. "You. Only you."

I stared at his swollen lips and glassy eyes, my chest feeling tight and funny, as if a pile of feathers had been released, churning madly against my ribcage.

Allowing him time to adjust to my cock, I plunged forward in shallow jabs. Callum muttered senselessly, the tip of his cock purple and leaking against his abdomen.

Gripping his length, I pumped up and down in a steady pace, as I marveled at how our bodies fit so seamlessly. I shuddered at the sensation of his narrow hole sheathing my shaft.

"Fuck me, Dean." His eyes had transformed to a liquid gold and he worried his lip as if clinging to his last measure of control. "Harder. I need it. I need *you*."

Forcing his legs higher, I delivered exactly what he wanted. I thrust forward in a punishing rhythm, my balls slapping his ass, solidly connecting with that spot inside him that made his eyes roll back in his head.

Both of us were sweating and grunting and close to ripping apart at the seams. So fucking close.

"I don't know what the hell you've done to me." I was out of my mind with raw sensation, my back arching as I pounded him senseless. "I didn't expect to feel like this, to want you so damn much."

He reached for his cock and stroked it a few times, moaning, as his eyes latched onto mine. A second longer and his limbs locked tight, his mouth opening on a soundless gasp, as he soared over the edge of the mountainside.

My rhythm faltered as I watched him, his hole narrowing around my cock, his muscles twitching.

"Ah, fuck." My entire body shuddered as I yelled out his name and came with a roar, my orgasm hitting me like a freight train, screeching through a black and starless night.

I collapsed on top of him, unable to hold myself up any longer as my cock slipped from his ass and I muttered into his neck, "So good, so goddamn good."

Callum rolled us onto our sides as he kissed my jaw and cheeks and lips. I groped beneath his sac and thrust two fingers inside him, knowing how much he enjoyed that feeling of fullness.

"Hell yes," he hissed in my ear, and then sucked on the skin right below, sure to leave a mark.

As our breathing stabilized, the stark reality settled atop us like a heavy blanket, prickly and cloying.

In near desperation, my fingers fumbled for his groin where the majority of his come had pooled. I swirled my fingers through the stickiness before swiping a line of his seed across my lips. Finding the pulse at my throat, I pressed the remainder into my skin, hoping for some of that magic he had talked about.

Eyes wide, his palm connected with my neck and he hauled me into a penetrating kiss that was brutal in its intensity. His tongue slipped inside and tasted every corner of my mouth, from gums, to palate, to teeth as if memorizing every last piece of me.

When we broke apart, we didn't speak—couldn't. As his fingers clutched my face, his parting words were narrated through his shattering gaze.

I wanted to shut my lids tight, to not remember how he was looking at me. It would hurt like a bitch tomorrow but I kept staring back. I needed to. All I had left was this moment.

After we cleaned up, he gently gathered me in his arms, intertwined our fingers and legs, and we slipped into sleep, however fitfully.

I woke intermittently throughout the night, peering through blurry eyes to be certain his solid form was still in my bed. To feel his heavy muscles, his soft breath.

When my phone alarm trilled me awake a few hours later, I whispered to him, "Coming with me?"

He groaned and turned over. "Not this time."

It was painstakingly difficult to leave that room but the run was the cold slap of reality I needed.

On my way home I went through the motions of ordering his coffee, knowing he'd already be gone.

As far as romantic sentiments went, his note was beautiful in its simplicity. Just like him.

I remembered the first day I had met Callum, how he had encouraged me to pick those wildflowers for his sister.

I might've known even then that he would touch me, teach me, and even walk away from me in a devastatingly important way.

DEAN,

I couldn't face you when I said goodbye.

Couldn't stare into those indigo eyes that remind me of the nighttime sky after sunset on the preserve.

How they call to my heart. Reach into my soul. See me just as I am.

I wish I could erase the color of your eyes from my head.

But I'm afraid they're permanently etched.

I meant everything I said about my family outside the bar last night.

If you need me—us—you'll know where to look.

Callum

37

DEAN

It'd been two months, five days, and thirteen hours since I'd last seen or heard from Callum.

I finished my final course and officially graduated with my master's degree—well, at least on paper. My parents called to congratulate me and invited me home for Thanksgiving, one of the few times they decided to stay put. I agreed, determined to speak to them face to face about a myriad of things. Maybe we could finally start building some kind of bridge.

After I let my new landlord know that I was all moved in, I slid into the driver's seat of my Mazda and got on the freeway, heading south on interstate ninety-five. Cassie and Professor Landon had been instrumental in assisting me with locating a decent apartment. But I was stretched thin due to helping Cassie with rent until she could make the move herself across a couple of states.

When I left town, Dermot had been up for a visit, so the goodbye had been easier. Besides, I'd see her again in a few weeks' time.

As I changed lanes, my thoughts drifted to Billie and how I'd sworn him to secrecy. We'd kept in contact quite a bit. He asked my advice about Leo, who had gone off to some private school in Florida. They would only see each other during holidays and though Billie was bummed, he knew he needed to focus on his health and his other friends.

He shared what a pain school could be in his small town, even though everybody knew about his condition. Didn't mean they were always cool about it. He'd turn sixteen in another month, and though he hadn't had another seizure since the summer, he knew he wouldn't be able to get his license unless he was in remission for much longer.

Billie had also helped me keep tabs on Callum. He told me that he'd decided to finish constructing what he described as a tiny cottage on the Shady Pines property. That his dad and Braden had helped him all summer long and he was already moved in.

I guess Callum had also been making more trips to the city to hang with Jason, but he didn't know if Callum was seeing anybody new. I actually didn't want that final piece of information, because it would've been too painful. I'd hoped that whoever did capture Callum's heart, that he'd keep it safe. Because I knew I would, if given the chance.

The familiar Shady Pines Preserve sign came into view, and I turned right, noticing a newly constructed roadside stand that was presently unoccupied. Cassie had told me about her family's plans to expand their reach and I figured she knew what she was talking about, after putting in so much effort behind that business degree.

When I pulled up to the main house Grammy and Billie were relaxing in the porch swing, and everything about that first day returned full force. Bullseye perked up to bark in my direction. As his dog approached the vehicle, recognition dawned on Billie's face.

As soon as I stepped out of the car, Billie was smiling and waving. I hadn't told him the day I'd be coming, only that it would be after the Lorrigans' alligator hunt, for obvious reasons. And as soon as I could muster the courage.

After I gave Billie a strong hug and Bullseye a good scratch behind the ears, I walked up the steps to greet Grammy. "It's good to see you, Dean."

"I figured I needed to check on that sugar cane field," I said, looking in the direction Billie and I had ridden so many weeks ago.

Grammy grinned and winked at me. "Callum's been taking pretty decent care of it, but he might need some extra supervising."

A blush crept across my cheeks. I breathed in the earthy air and nostalgia bloomed in my chest about being back here.

"He just got home, you know," Grammy said. "From a shrimping trip with his daddy in the gulf."

"Guess I timed it perfectly, then," I said, smiling.

"Head on back to his place," Grammy said. "You should know the way. It's just beyond the orchard."

"Okay," I said, suddenly feeling unsteady on my feet. "Near the field where Gus comes out at night?"

"Gus?" Billie asked and my blush deepened. "You know about Gus?"

Grammy cackled. "I trust he knows plenty more than you think he does."

I simply shook my head and started walking toward the garage, passing the hearty vegetable garden along the way. The sweet citrus scent from the orchard wafted up my nose.

Just beyond the fig tree that Grammy used for her preserves was a clearing. I stopped in my tracks taking it all in. Callum's home was about the size of a singlewide trailer, same rectangular shape as well. Except it was constructed of dark wood with a cream-colored door and window boxes planted with wildflowers that added a homey touch.

I stepped closer to the house, my pulse pounding at my

throat. I smelled the aroma of the blossoms before plucking off a bright yellow bud and heading to the front entrance.

After I knocked, I couldn't help fidgeting as I waited for Callum to answer the door. His hair was a mess of red tangles, most likely from his favorite ball cap, and his cheekbones were sun streaked from the ocean.

His amber eyes widened, his fingers gripping the doorframe. "Dean, what—"

My brain fumbling through what I wanted to say, I thrust the yellow flower in his direction and then dug in my pocket for the envelope I needed to give him as well.

"This place looks amazing," I said, as he sniffed at the bud absently.

When I handed him the white folded paper, our fingers brushed, and I bit down on my trembling lip.

"What's this?" he asked, his eyebrows knitting in complete bewilderment.

"I, uh, wanted to invite you to a Yankees training game. Their pre-season camp is in Tampa, you know," I said, and then shook my head. "Of course you do. Damn it, sorry."

The corner of his lip lifted, possibly recounting our last fight about me *schooling* him, and his amused expression helped my shoulders unwind.

"Billie said you've never been to a pre-season or regular season game," I said and he looked over my shoulder as if putting two and two together that his brother and I had been communicating. "Anyway, the first game is in March and I wondered if you'd go with me."

He flipped the envelope open and glanced at the tickets inside. "That's five months from now."

"Right. So, you know," I said, kicking at a stone on the ground. "Depending on what you decide, you can just as easily take somebody else."

"What I decide?" he said, arching his eyebrow.

"I've read your note about a thousand times," I mumbled as sweat broke out across my brow. "And I have things I need to say to you."

"Okay," he said, his eyes burrowing into mine, leaving me winded.

"I...well..." Unexpected tears misted my eyes. "I'm in love with you. And..."

Fuck, I needed to pull it together. I took a deep breath and continued baring my soul. "And I thought if you haven't moved on...if you still feel anything for me...maybe we could date and see where that leads us."

It felt like an eternity had passed before Callum said anything. He stood motionless staring at me, a ghost of a smile on his lips. Finally, he stepped forward and ran his fingers beneath my jaw.

I shut my eyes at the feel of his skin brushing against mine.

"Damn," he said. "Are you really standing here in front of me?"

Opening my lids I inhaled roughly. He was so darn close I could feel his soft breath against my cheek.

"I missed you," I said, in nearly a whimper.

He moved nearer, the warmth from his heated skin whispering over the hairs on my arms, generating a subtle tremor.

"I missed you *more*," he murmured and then swiped his lips across mine. "And I love you, too."

My body sagged against his. Curling my fingers around his nape to tighten our connection, I kissed him with all that I had. When his tongue slipped inside my mouth, it felt like coming home.

I moaned as he gripped my shirt and pulled me so close there was scarcely any space between us. His one arm wound around my waist and the other tightened in my hair and I could feel his cock plumping against my own. It had been too damn long.

He dragged his lips away, but kept our foreheads together, as we panted into each other's mouths. "How...how did you get here? Is Cassie—"

"I live in Florida now," I said and the words gave me pause. Whoa. I officially resided in a southern state for the first time in my life. I'd miss the spring and fall and the summer heat was bound to kill me, but I wanted to give it a fair shot.

"What?" Callum sputtered, blinking at me.

"Professor Landon offered me a research position in his lab," I said. "We'll be studying immunology and metagenomics to further comprehend the microbial communities as related to plants."

As his lip pinched into a smirk, I didn't even care if he was poking fun at me. Not this time. Callum was smart, beautiful, and passionate. I was madly in love and I wanted him to be mine. All mine.

"I'll be living in an apartment about forty minutes away and I thought maybe..."

He drew me into a scorching kiss, his tongue delving deep in my mouth.

"I'm so fucking happy you're here," he said against my lips and then led me by the hand into his new home. I scarcely had a second to take in the modern fixtures and the cozy decor before he steered me up the stairs to his sizeable loft bed.

"This place has solar panels and will only leave a small environmental footprint," he said, nudging me down in his soft sheets. "I thought you might appreciate that."

"That must mean you've been thinking about me?" I asked, staring up at him from lowered lashes.

Callum sank down and his body covered mine. I sighed at the weight of him, the smell of pine, along with a hint of saltwater from his trip. "Every single day."

Our lips fused and our hands groped, barely able to break apart long enough to remove our shirts and pants, so that we could finally be skin to skin.

"I missed this," he said as he tugged our boxers down. As soon as our hard cocks aligned and rubbed, we both moaned. Callum kissed me so thoroughly that my mouth ached for more. "Missed your lips and your eyes."

"You haven't tried to get out there—" I could barely even finish the thought. But I needed to know he was certain, ready... for everything. With me. "I thought maybe you needed—"

His head jerked back and the look he gave me left me breathless. "Only wanted you."

We rutted against each other, our lips never parting, our bodies wound tight.

Callum reached between us and wrapped his large hand around both of our cocks.

"Didn't know how I was supposed to get over you," I said, thrusting into his palm.

"Fuck," he groaned. "Need you so much. Don't need anybody else."

We came at nearly the same time, panting and shuddering, the sheets twisted around our legs. I held onto him, our come mixing together, unwilling to let go this time.

After cleaning up, we lay side by side staring up at the ceiling, which boasted an impressive skylight.

"You can see the stars from here," he said, his thumb tracing over my palm in a mesmerizing pattern. "Pictured you with me just like this."

I pulled Callum into a kiss that made him groan against me and only removed my tongue from his mouth when we needed air. My heart was full to bursting point and everything felt so fucking perfect.

We heard barking outside along with the sound of a motor. Quickly slipping into our clothes, we headed out the door.

"Sorry," Billie said from his four-wheeler. "I promised Grammy I'd give you more time. Was hoping you'd want to go for a ride?"

"Always." I beamed at him so wide my cheeks hurt. "Will you take me to see the sugar canes?"

Callum mounted the other vehicle parked beside his house and fired up the engine. "Let's go."

I climbed on the back of the leather seat, and wound my arms around his stomach, which quivered at my touch. As we rode, I buried my face in his shirt, smelling him, just wanting to be close any way I could. Callum's fingers kept slipping over mine as if needing the same kind of contact.

At the field, I hopped off and walked up and down the rows happy to already see some growth. "Looks good."

"Now that you're here you can help keep it thriving," Billie said. "You will be around...won't you?"

Billie looked so encouraged right then that I threw my arm around his shoulders.

My eyes darted to Callum to be certain we were on the same page. His sexy grin was so gorgeous I nearly lost my breath. "I'll definitely be around."

A familiar noise resonated in the distance and my eyes widened in wonder.

It was Grammy ringing the dinner bell. The sound was as comforting as a worn pair of jeans.

Callum's eyes lit up and he delivered a chaste kiss to my lips. "Want to stay for supper?"

"I'd love to," I said, my heart in my throat. "As long as there's no alligator or rattlesnake on the menu."

Billie and Callum exchanged glances and then burst out laughing. My chest squeezed as I studied the pair of handsome brothers, who seemed closer than ever.

"How do you feel about shrimp?" Callum asked, his eyebrow quirked.

"You coming?" Billie asked impatiently as he got himself situated on his ATV. Bullseye ran in circles around him, having recognized the chiming alert as well.

"We can't keep Grammy waiting," Callum said, yanking my arm toward the four-wheeler. "She'll tan our behinds."

I couldn't keep the smile off my face as I climbed behind Callum, gripped him tight, and delivered a wet kiss to his nape.

It felt like we were riding off into the sunset. Creating our own kind of happy.

THANK YOU for reading THE DEEPEST BLUE!

I hope you enjoyed it!

Reviews help other readers find books. So if you feel compelled one way or another to leave a sentence or two on a retail site, I appreciate it!

Read on to view a short excerpt from the next book in the Roadmap series, The Hardest Fall, which takes us to New York City.

ABOUT THE AUTHOR

ONCE UPON A TIME, I lived in New York City and was a wardrobe stylist. I spent my days getting in cabs, shopping for photo shoots, eating amazing food, and drinking coffee at my favorite hangouts.

Now I live in the Midwest with my husband and son—my two favorite guys. I've been a clinical social worker and a special education teacher. But it wasn't until I wrote a weekly column for the local newspaper that I realized I could turn the fairytales inside my head into the reality of writing fiction.

I'm addicted to lip balm and salted caramel everything. I write Adult, New Adult, and M/M Contemporary Romance. I also believe in true love and kissing, so writing romance novels has become a dream job.

Standalone:

Love Me Louder

There You Stand

Beautiful Dreamer

MMM with Felice Stevens:

Last Call

First Light

Under My Skin series

Regret

Reawaken

Reclaim

Redeem

Co-written with Nyrae Dawn (AKA Riley Hart):

Free Fall series:

TOUCH THE SKY

CHASE THE SUN

PAINT THE STARS

Spinoff from Free Fall series:

LIVING OUT LOUD

Standalone:

EVER AFTER: A GAY FAIRY TALE

Forever Moore: A Gay Fairy Tale

Roadmap to Your Heart series

The Darkest Flame

The Faintest Spark

The Deepest Blue

The Hardest Fall

The Sweetest Goodbye

M/F books that can all standalone:

All of You

Before You Break

Whisper to Me

Promise Me This

Two of Hearts

Three Sacred Words

Twelve Truths and a Lie

ACKNOWLEDGMENTS

To Stina, Nyrae, Keyanna, Edie, Melinda, Lori, Judy, and Kanaxa —for helping make this book shine.

To Greg and Evan, for not complaining when I have to disappear to work at odd hours of any random day. I don't want to be in any other place in the world except right next to you, every single night.

To my family and friends for your constant, unwavering support. I love you.

To the amazing book bloggers and reviewers out there—there are too many of you to list here. Please just know I appreciate all the work you do—all on your own dime—for the simple love of books. Because when it comes down to it, all of us are readers first and foremost.

Last, to the readers: THANK YOU for taking a chance on my books and reaching out to talk to me about them. For an author, there may be no better feeling.

EXCERPT FROM THE HARDEST FALL

TATE

My arm shot up and I pointed at the ceiling as I belted out the last note of a Gaga song. If I had her voice, I'd be rolling in the millions instead of lip-synching her pop tunes, wearing heavy purple eye shadow, and silver stilettos that pinched my freaking toes.

But I had a blast performing as Frieda Love, I was damn good at it, and the stage adored me. As did the crowd, if a couple dozen gay men wolf whistling had anything to say about it. Or that sexy man in the corner whose dark eyes tracked me two nights a week.

Dark Eyes looked straight as they come with his perfectly tailored button-front shirt that opened at the throat, exposing a patch of smooth tan skin and a fine silver chain. But plenty of het men and women came into Ruby Redd's Bar and Grille. Some stayed for the food, others for the entertainment.

As I exited the stage down the three steps to the dance floor, I spotted Dean and Callum near the bar. Making my way through a sea of bodies, fingers groped and voices carried as the audience congratulated me on a great performance. Frieda Love might screw around with one of her regulars tonight, but first I wanted to hang out with my friends.

"*Girl*," Jessica, one of the other queens who had already performed tonight, drawled in my ear. "You looked ridiculously fab up there."

Hazel Nuts, as she was known on stage, was in transition, drop dead gorgeous, and had a huge following in this crowd as well. Fuck the prejudice she encountered in her everyday life from the asshats that couldn't see how radiant she was in her own skin.

Here at Ruby Redd's we were strictly against the use of such language as *tranny* and *shemale*, which were not only derogatory but also encouraged the idea that transsexuals were men dressed as women. Any hecklers were immediately thrown out on their asses because the owner, Maurice, ran a tight ship.

I kissed her cheek as I walked by. "Thanks, sexy. My friends are waiting at the bar."

I hadn't seen Dean since he graduated from NC State last fall. He looked good, especially with Callum standing behind him with his burly arms wrapped around his waist and his face nuzzled in his neck. Dean and Callum were really good together and I couldn't be happier for them.

They were only in town so Callum could finally meet Dean's parents in Jersey. While here they had also planned to visit me and to see a Yankee game, since Callum was a huge fan.

I was back in the city because I didn't have many other options. This was my hometown, my mother lived on the Upper East Side with her new husband, and I was having trouble finding full-time employment.

It took me two additional years to graduate from NC State with a communications degree because some of the credits wouldn't transfer from NYU. Broadcasting jobs were hard to come by and though I had interned at an online publication there were no openings available at the time. I stayed as long as I could before finally coming home.

Now I did what I knew best—performed as drag queen extraordinaire at a bar on Christopher Street two nights a week. That, along with my graphic T-shirt business helped me contribute to the rent in the small West Village apartment I shared with my best friend, Tori.

"I always knew you could rock the stage," Callum said in his southern drawl as soon as I reached them. He looked so much more comfortable in his own skin then he had six months ago, which was really cool to witness.

"Of course I can." I spun around and shook my booty in my white beaded dress while they cracked up. I made sure not to bend too low and rip the seam because the cost of dressing in drag was not for the faint of heart. I went for demure Gaga tonight because her elaborate costumes broke the bank, probably even for her. Besides, I wasn't a fan of wearing meat, only packing it.

A man from a nearby table whistled at me and I recognized the dude after he slipped me a twenty at the end of my performance. The way he eyed me now told me he was hoping for some Frieda loving tonight, but I wasn't someone who could be bought. Still, I could flirt shamelessly with the best of them.

I hugged Dean and then turned toward the tall and hulking Callum to wind my arms around his shoulders. I couldn't help sniffing his cologne extra deep since he was plain gorgeous and just the kind of guy I got a boner for.

"That's long enough," Dean hissed in my direction. "Stop mauling my man."

"You mean I can't sneak in an ass grab?" I quipped before backing away. Seeing that possessive look in my friend's eye was humorous, but also gave me an ache in my chest that I couldn't quite explain. I didn't want to explore what that meant, so I brushed it aside.

When I glanced over Callum's shoulder the same man with the dark eyes and inky black hair was watching me and once he was caught staring, his gaze flitted away.

Maybe he appreciated the make-up, the blonde wig. I'd been told I had a nice jawline and could pull off my female counterpart pretty convincingly. Dark Eyes was probably a straight guy who enjoyed the female anatomy, even though my boobs were falsies, same as my eyelashes. Maybe he'd even been with a couple of queens who were asked to stay in full costume while he pounded them from behind so he could maintain his het status in his own deluded mind.

My gut tightened painfully remembering being in just such a precarious position.

I wondered how he'd react if I approached him without the getup, with a fresh face, clean of makeup. My bet was that he'd run in the other direction. Fucker.

He wasn't exactly my type so what the hell did I care? He might've been a bit taller and thicker than me but he matched me in build, with his solid shoulders and lean waist. He had a beautifully masculine face, not boyish in the least, with a strong brow and full lips. Compared to my blond hair and fair skin, we'd be quite the contrast.

But his eyes were the draw for me, especially when I was on stage. How they tracked me, made me wonder what he was thinking. They were soulful, a cross between forlorn and world-weary, and though I really had no patience for emo guys, for some reason the more I saw him the more curious I became.

"So what's new?" I asked the gorgeous couple standing in front of me, breaking my gaze from the mysterious man who did not deserve so much of my attention.

"Mom and Dad are warming up to Callum," Dean said, grasping for his guy's hand. "They're glad I brought home a *friend*."

"Friend?" I scoffed. "Seriously?"

"They're slowly coming around," Dean said. "Especially after our argument on Thanksgiving when I told them they'd be losing another son if they didn't accept me for who I am."

"His mom kind of lost it," Callum supplied, after sipping from his glass. "Got herself together right quick. Called him and told him she wanted to be part of his life."

"Damn straight." I clapped Dean on the shoulder.

"And how's business?" I asked Callum because his family owned a hunting preserve in small town hick-country Florida.

"Doing great," he said, taking another pull of his beer. I realized how parched I was from performing as I watched him swallow. It had nothing to do with that enticing Adam's apple bobbing up and down.

"He's been making all kinds of furniture and his family is selling sugar cane syrup," Dean said, looking at his boy with pride.

"Cassie and Billie?" I knew his sister Cassie from NC State and heard his brother had a therapy dog that assisted him with his seizure disorder. But that he was also wicked smart, loved to bake, and hadn't yet officially come out to his family.

"Cassie is engaged to Dermot," he said. "And Billie begged to come to the city with us. I told him next time for sure because he's still in school."

"That kid has wanderlust." I grinned. "Maybe he'll decide to leave that town."

Something gloomy passed through Callum's gaze. I knew how protective he was of his brother.

"He could study abroad or attend culinary school," I suggested. "Have him come to the city. I'll look out for him."

Dean's eyes bugged out and Callum burst out laughing.

"Thanks for the vote of confidence," I huffed out, crossing my arms over my boobs, which felt like they'd shifted a bit during my performance. "I wouldn't let him get into any trouble. I'd slowly introduce him to the scene."

Just because I would never settle down didn't mean I couldn't be a good friend to somebody who needed support. I certainly would never want anybody to get burned the way I did. Gay dudes who pretended to be super straight to the detriment of everybody around them could go suck it.

That includes you, Dark Eyes. I could feel his heated gaze on me again. Bet his thumb was fingering the condensation on the glass. Gin and tonic with lime every single visit. I could ask the bartender who was scheduled most nights I was on stage. Phil always had a tall glass of water with lemon waiting at the bar for me after my performances. He would tell me if Dark Eyes was batting for the same team or if he seemed to swing both ways. But then I'd appear desperate, and queens were never desperate. We always had plenty of men to hold court.

"Let me get changed," I said, reaching for the cold liquid on the bar but refusing to look in Dark Eyes' direction again. "My feet are killing me, but I want to watch Candy Cane perform."

Dean pulled Callum toward the dance floor and then locked him in a kiss that made my toes curl. Well, fuck. I threw Dark Eyes one final glance as I sipped at the water and bit down on an ice cube. I would definitely find somebody to hook up with tonight. Somebody who was eager for a piece of this fine ass.

Just as I had the thought, one of my regulars crowded my personal space and made the motion to kiss my cheek before I had the sense to back away. How dare he think he could touch this queen without her consent?

"You were spectacular tonight," he mumbled with glazed eyes. He was already half-crocked, so I let him off the hook this time. Nothing worse than a sloppy fuck.

"Frieda Love always brings her A game," I cooed to him over my shoulder. "Better get yourself a cab ride home."

Made in the USA
Middletown, DE
08 July 2021